ONE KNIFE
MANY LIVES

by

Anthony L. Olaseinde

COPYRIGHT

Cover Design: Raheem Currie | Blessed
Illustrations: Dean Rogan | Partial Artist
Editor: Kirsten Rees | MakeMeASuccess

ISBN: 978-1-83804-990-4

DEDICATION

This book is dedicated to all those who have had the unfortunate and unpleasant experience of being affected by knife crime. It is also to those who feel they need to carry a knife. Do not do it, it's not worth it. You have been blessed with life, so make the most of it. I am dyslexic and I don't even have a Level 4 (C) GCSE in English. I think I got a Level 2 (E) both times, yet I wrote a book. Trust me when I tell you, the only thing between you and your goals is you.

THE EPIGRAPH

You can either do it because you WANT to or do it because you HAVE to do it. The thing is, when you WANT to, you have the choice to do it your way. So why wait until you have no other choice.

– Anthony L. Olaseinde

CHAPTERS

PREFACE

I have done so much work on knife crime over these past three years and the hardest part for me, is trying to get people to realise it can happen to anyone. It really upsets me when they are adamant that their child won't feel the impact, like they have the power to choose if they become a victim or not.

When I talk to people about their deceased relative or friend who has been taken away through knife crime, every single one of them say the same thing, 'I didn't think it would happen to me'. Unfortunately, it is too late then, their loved one has already gone. We should be proactive, we should pull together and spread awareness, sparing more families the heartache. The purpose of this book is to show the heart-breaking trail of destruction knife crime leaves behind. Although this book is fictional, the dangers of knife crime are VERY REAL.

FOLLOW THE JOURNEY

Always An Alternative:

Website: www.alwaysanalternative.org.uk

Instagram: @aaamindset

Facebook: Always An Alternative

Email: info@alwaysanalternative.org.uk

Author:

Instagram: @antzjourney

Twitter: @antzjourney

Facebook: Big Ant

ACKNOWLEDGEMENTS

Thank you to Lauren and our beautiful children Masen and Gracie, for listening to me every time I wrote a new chapter or added one thousand words. My Nan, Lol for always being so supportive and reminding me it was my book, therefore, my rules and Joanne for being my voluntary personal assistant and reminding me of the difference it will make.

Shout out to Dean for doing the chapter illustrations, Raheem for the cover design, and Amy for the promotional graphics.

Finally, thank you to all of the people I have met though my anti-knife campaign #KEEP SHEFFIELD STAINLESS and my not-for-profit company, Always An Alternative.

WE WILL MAKE A DIFFERENCE!

ONE

YOUNG, FRESH AND SCARED

"What you sayin' tonight, are you about?" asked Kiki.

"You know this," Sean replied with a hint of assurance.

"You still coming to the house party around the corner from mine though?"

In a stern voice, Sean said, "I'm not repeating myself."

Both Sean and Kiki burst into laughter. Sean covered his mouth like he had bad breath.

"Okay, okay I'll see you there," Sean said as he continued to laugh.

He ended the call and continued scrolling through his social media platform, picture after picture. Pictures of exotic food, fast cars, and expensive jewellery but none of the images were able to catch his attention. However, the music introducing the latest headline on the news did.

"We have saddening news to report to you this evening," the news reporter announced before pausing momentarily to show his empathy.

From the neck down, Sean's body paused. Only his head turned to view what was about to be shown on the screen of his sleek, black, 42-inch smart TV.

"Another victim of knife crime: a teenager stabbed to death."

The coldness in the news reporter's voice brought a bitter feeling into the room, making him shiver, as if something ran through him. He adjusted in his posture, feeling uncomfortable. As if Sean were not aware of the seriousness of this incident, the coldness could not take a hold of him, the bitterness could not yet reach his heart.

"What a waste," he said, shaking his head.

After a moment, his eyes flicked back to his phone. His thumb swiped up, eyes roaming down the feed. Scroll. Scroll. Stop. His focus was pinpointed like an archer ready to fire their arrow at a target, his attention now fully consumed. The top of his thumb shook, hovering over the screen. His eyes studied every part of the picture in granular detail. The background was full of people holding drinks, laughing, joking, and dancing. The lighting was low but in the forefront was a girl who was glowing.

It was her face that had stopped him scrolling but the stunning bright red strapless dress certainly deserved attention too. It stopped just above the knee, revealing her slim, smooth, silky legs. Sean placed his index finger and thumb on the phone screen and pulled them apart, the image zoomed passed the username H4NN4H and focused on her face.

"She is so beautif -".

The picture vanished.

His phone vibrated, the shock causing him to drop the phone. It bounced across the soft grey carpet before landing face down underneath his freshly made bed. While Sean's heart was still beating rapidly, he scurried on to his hands and knees, to pick his phone up before the call stopped.

He made it, it was Kiki, telling him that Hannah would be at the party. Sean had always played it cool by acting like he did not know why Hannah was so important. But Kiki was no fool, she picked up on the way they looked at each other. Their stares, once locked on to each other, it was unbreakable. Just as unbreakable as his smile every time he walked away, beaming from ear to ear.

Sean cut the conversation short. He did not want Kiki to find out they had been seeing each other for over ten months. The couple decided they would not tell anyone about their relationship as they did not want people interfering and trying to ruin it. They both agreed on the quote, 'All good things come to an end,'. But they were willing to do all they could to preserve their love for each other; true love.

Sean ran upstairs to get showered. Once in the bathroom, he placed his phone on the dark granite windowsill and got undressed.

"SWOOOSH," he shouted, throwing his dirty clothes in the white wash basket like it was a basketball through a hoop.

The water from the shower pounded Sean's head like it was a jet wash. He found it therapeutic, allowing him to slip into deep thoughts about his future. *Should we make our relationship known? Will I get a scholarship at NASA? Is this party even worth it?*

4

"Oh jheeez, the party!"

With no hesitation, Sean turned the shower off and grabbed his towel from the chrome-heated towel rack. After drying his front, he gripped the towel and dried his back in a flossing action. Wrapping the towel around his waist, he headed out of the bathroom and made his way down the hallway to his bedroom.

A crisp, white t-shirt freshly ironed greeted him when he entered his room.

"Thanks Mum," he said, even though she could not hear him.

He opened the wardrobe door and pulled his clothes across the clothing rail like a high speed train passing by. As his hand touched the shoulder of his grey Nike tracksuit, he reminisced on the compliments he had received whilst wearing it. However, he did not like it for how it looked on, he liked it for the softness of the material when it touched his skin. He felt comfort every time contact was made between his skin and the tracksuit. This would definitely keep him warm all night.

Sitting on the edge of his bed he reached his arm underneath and pulled out a brown cardboard box, with a huge Nike tick on it. Inside were a pair of brand-new, un-creased Air Force Ones: the soles so clean he could have eaten off of them. He slid both feet into the trainers and jumped up off his bed like a jack in a box. He walked to the mirror like he had a stone in his trainer.

Whilst looking at himself in the mirror he raised his right eyebrow, pouted his lips, and rubbed his hands together in a way that resembled an evil villain in a movie. Catching his own eye, he realised how stupid he looked. Laughing at himself, he sat on the end of his bed and threw his upper body back onto his bed, throwing his hands up into the air like an inflatable man, hitting the bed with a bounce.

As Sean lay there looking into space, his phone lit up, it was Kiki again. He let it ring, finally picking up with a sigh on the fourth ring.

"Yo Sean, have you heard?"

Looking puzzled at the phone, he replied, "Heard what?"

"About Daniel, yo."

"Nah, why, what's up?" he replied swiftly.

"He got got man, he got chinged up."

"Stop your noise, you're chatting."

"Trust me, his sister told me directly."

Kiki kept talking but he could not take it in, his thoughts were a blur.

6

He felt the hairs on his arms stand up straight, his skin broke out in goose bumps. Sean's body was in conflict. Breathing, fighting with speaking. His brain trying to find sense. The conflict manifested for around thirty seconds and ended in a deep breath and a sigh: no words could be found.

"Sean, Sean," said Kiki, trying to get through to him.

He tuned back in to her voice, to her words.

"He's okay. They got him at the hospital. It was serious but he'll live.

Kiki went on to tell him who did it and why.

Sean ended the call and stared into space, his reaction was different when being compared to when he watched the news about the person that had lost his life earlier on in the day. The news of his friend hit him hard, it was far too close to home. The attack was done by some-one they all knew, Kyle, not a friend, more of an acquaintance. It did not add up, the at-tacker was just a 'wannabe gangster' and the victim, Daniel, a nice guy who joked around all the time.

Sean had memories of Kyle being beat up by girls and distinctly remembered the high-pitched yelp Kyle made when running off. Still puzzled, Sean could not comprehend the attack when he found out the reason: a disagreement over a football result. How was that a justifiable reason to stab someone?

They knew each other, each other's parents. We all used to chill. It means nothing, Daniel could have lost his life! he thought.

Sean sat back up on the edge of his bed and put his head into his hands. He could not understand how someone could potentially take a life over a disagreement, there is no need. Sean scratched his head as if he scratched enough an answer would appear, but it did not. The answer is so much bigger than him.

Knife crime has been on the rise for years in the country leaving a path of devastation: 285 murders and 5,149 hospital admissions the previous years. The government had made poor attempts to resolve this deep-rooted issue. The first attempt was increasing stop and search powers for police. This solution weakened the relationship between the police and the communities as they felt it would lead to black and ethnic people of minority getting harassed by police. It did, but most importantly it did not yield any real results.

The other attempt was to give funding to charities, this move was more the government trying to shift the responsibility away from them. As predicted, it failed miserably as the well-known charities won the funding, but they did not reach the right people, the ones at risk of knife crime. Not to knock those smaller charities and campaigners, they were playing their part and making their mark. Unfortunately, it was only scratching the surface.

Parents were struggling due to a new roll out of a benefits system, so any extra money was being spent on necessities. Young people have nowhere to go and nothing to do, leaving them vulnerable to being exploited by criminal gangs. Unfortunately, this was only heightening the risk of young people being involved in criminal activities to make money.

Sean was living in this dangerous time and could easily end up a statistic. And although he was not into the politics, he understood the issues and felt that he had the answer.

He thought of a youth club, a safe place provided for young people. Where they could relax, socialise, and learn new skills without the risk of being exploited by criminal gangs.

Additionally, by having mentors to work with young people, they would have real role models to inspire them to progress in life, thus deterring them from hanging around on the street.

He sighed loudly, wishing he could make it happen, but he knew there was nothing he could do. Pushing himself up from the bed and headed out his room.

Shaking off the bad news, he stood up and headed for the door. Running down the stairs as if it were a race, Sean shouted bye to his mother before leaping from the fourth step and landing with a thud. He opened the door to the closet to grab a coat.

"Finally," he whispered under his breath, clenching his fist as if he were celebrating.

The weather was cold enough for him to wear his new coat. He was bursting at the seams to show it off. It was knee-length and filled with feathers, making it look puffy, like a new pillow. The hood to the chest was a shiny vibrant orange. The chest down was dark grey, almost black.

His arms slid smoothly into the coat, leaving a touch of room for growth. As he pulled the zip up from the knees, he noticed the tags were still on the coat. He went back into the kitchen to get the scissors to cut it off.

Opening the drawer, all Sean saw were knives staring back at him. In the background, he heard the theme song to the news and remembered the person being stabbed to death earlier that day. His thoughts were then brought to Daniel being stabbed, the reason for it, and the person who did the senseless stabbing.

Sean's heart began to beat faster, he felt worried and suddenly found it difficult to breathe. Unexpectedly, he had an overwhelming feeling of death. Questions sprung into his mind out of nowhere; *Who is going to be at the party? Will they have knives? Will they use them? What if Hannah is there? The feeling of death took over Sean's body like a fever.* His anxiety was at a high, as he reached into the drawer and picked up a small kitchen knife with a black handle.

Cutting the tag off, his hand hovered above the drawer ready to put the knife back. But he retracted his hand.

"I think I'll take this, just in case."

Tucking the knife into the waistband of his tracksuit bottoms, his heartbeat slowed, and his anxieties flew away like a scared bird. The knife brought him a sense of safety, a sense of security, a sense of protection.

TWO

WE ALL HAVE OUR PROBLEMS

Andrew placed the blue razor blade under the warm tap to wash away the excess shaving foam. He then turned the tap off and flicked his wrist sharply to rid the rest of the water, leaving the blade clean. Looking in the mirror he was greeted by his hairless face. Running his fingers across his smooth skin, he was finished.

Grabbing a bottle of his favourite cologne, Andrew sprayed it on his freshly shaved face. Bracing himself for what was coming, he clenched his teeth tightly together, almost causing them to fuse. The sting was intense, as the alcohol-based liquid touched the nicks and cuts made by the blade. He took an aggressive gasp through his teeth, sounding like the air gusting from a punctured tyre. A deep exhale followed shortly, which lasted until the pain from the sting became bearable.

"Andrew are you nearly ready? The taxi will be here in five," his wife, Kelly yelled from downstairs.

While buttoning up the last button on his blue designer shirt, Andrew replied, "I told you I will be ready."

He muttered an insult underneath his breath. Taking one last look in the mirror, he then made his way down the stairs.

A white Mercedes taxi arrived, the couple hopped in and were en route to a local Italian for their tenth-anniversary meal. Upon arrival, Kelly opened the heavy door to the restaurant; it was so heavy that she had to plant her feet firmly on the ground and push with all her might. A waiter noticed Kelly struggling through the glass door and went to her aid.

"Let me help you with that, Bellissima."

Rather than helping his wife, Andrew fixed a look on Kelly like she was a piece of dirt on his shoe. She recognised this glance, lowering her head and stared at the floor as she shuffled in the door whispering 'thank you' to the waiter.

You could see the entire restaurant from the entrance. It was beautiful. The ceiling was low, hanging from it were glass light shades, attached to the cables by brushed brass housing. Green vines climbed up two white walls toward the light. The other walls were chipped back to raw red bricks and housed black and white pictures from old Italy, capturing cars, people, and buildings. White marble tiles covered the floor, black streaks ran through them perfectly, it looked like juice mixed with water.

All the tables and chairs were covered in white material. Each table was home to a small glass vase with a freshly cut red rose placed inside. It was buzzing and the atmosphere was so welcoming. The couple were greeted by a man in a white shirt, black tie, and black waistcoat.

"Good evening Madam, Sir, how may I help?" the middle-aged waiter asked in a welcoming tone.

Kelly gave their details but unfortunately, there had been a mistake. The restaurant had doubled booked their reservation. Before the waiter could explain the mishap, Andrew got very aggressive and started using vulgar language attracting the attention of the manager who rushed over.

"Sir, can you refrain from using that language in our restaurant."

"What are you talking about, you messed up our table."

"Okay, I see why you are upset. But I will not accept that behaviour in our restaurant."

In a threatening manner, Andrew stepped up to the manager and said, "Well what are you going to do about it, boss man?"

The manager stepped back replying, "I am deeply sorry for the mix up here. I will upgrade your table and give you a complimentary bottle of our house wine."

"Thank you," said Kelly.

Andrew could not handle the way the manager did not rise to his aggression, so he stormed off to the toilet. Kelly felt so embarrassed, so ashamed. She could not apologise enough for her husband's disgusting behaviour. All she could do was give the staff an apologetic smile.

The door on the men's toilet opened with a huge bang. Andrew pushed it with so much force it nearly detached from its hinges as it hit the wall. Customers sat with pricked ears as the thud of the door attracted their attention. As it closed behind him, Andrew opened his wallet and pulled out a clear bag, it looked like a doggy bag but smaller. Within the bag was a small white rock, no bigger than a sugar cube.

He lifted the bag towards his nose and inhaled deeply, as if he could smell the substance through the sealed plastic bag. After clenching it in the palm of his hand, he traced his thumb down past his mouth, neck, and stopped at the centre of his chest. Clenching his grip harder, the rock broke and Andrew tilted his head towards the heavens as if the substance in the bag was an answer from above to all his problems.

Before Andrew had the chance to thank whatever powers from above granted him such an escape, his problems came calling. He swiftly made his way to a cubical and locked the door behind him. He opened the bag and the larger rock tumbled out followed by a few smaller rocks, like an avalanche the rocks sat on top of the toilet basin. He pulled a red card from his wallet, placed it on top of the biggest rock and applied pressure. It soon collapsed into a group of smaller rocks.

The side of the card then came crashing down on the smaller rocks, making a tapping sound on the hard toilet basin; like a starving man tapping his knife and fork on the table waiting for his favourite meal. Rocks no more, the substance covered the surface like snow. Andrew used the card to separate it into four equal lines.

Andrew took a rolled-up five-pound note, put it up his nose and hovered above the lines momentarily, before proceeding to snort. The rolled-up note followed the lines like a footballer on the wing of a football pitch. After the final line, again, Andrew tilted his head up to the sky. However, this time he raised his hands above his head: his problems momentarily hidden, and his answers found.

Heading back to the entrance, Andrew felt calm, fresh, and full of confidence; totally forgetting about the incident with the table. With a spring in his step, he walked right past Kelly.

"Andrew, they've sat us here," Kelly shouted but in a whisper. "Are you okay? You were ages in the toilet," she asked in a worried tone.

Andrew shrugged it off, blamed it on a sandwich he had eaten at work. She knew this was not the truth but smiled her usual empathetic little smile.

The couple ordered their starters, prawns and monkfish soup for Kelly, while Andrew went with Calamari. While waiting, they reminisced on their years of marriage. The first property they purchased, was a fifth-floor flat in a very rough part of town. There were always drug users coming and going around their block.

Lifeless, zombie-like people trying to sell anything they could touch with their dirty fingers. Kelly rarely thought about their old place, preferring not to think about the rancid smell which made its mark on any nose it had the pleasure of gracing. If the smell were a character it would be the evilest which, one that nobody would approach. Similar to the intimidating gang of drug dealers, which made the stairwells a no-go zone at night, forcing pedestrians to hide as the sun did. Andrew, on the other hand, would often reminisce, as if he liked to remind her of how good they had it now.

The view out of the rear of the flat was truly spectacular. During the day you could see as far as the eye would allow. In the night, the hustle and bustle of the city illuminated the picturesque view. There was a sense of pride in that flat, it was their home, it was where their child was born. While sharing the moment of their appreciation for the five-bedroom detached house they have now, the waiter came to serve their starter.

The food looked spectacular, the prawn and monkfish soup came in a small, flat, round steel pan with handles. The pieces of prawn and chunks of monkfish raised above the tomato soup, like stones when the tide goes out. The dried dill dressing finished the dish off perfectly. It smelled so rich and full of flavour. The calamari were deep fried to perfection, golden brown and topped with basil leaves and a piece of lemon on the side. It smelled so fresh, like it was caught from the sea and served in a restaurant on the seafront of Italy's coast.

The waiter put Kelly's plate down softly, you could not even hear it touch the cloth. With a smile, he said, "Here you go, my love".

The waiter then turned to Andrew and tossed his calamari at him, like it was rubbish destined for the bin. The waiter clearly upset by Andrew's actions at the start of the night. Looking straight in his eyes, the waiter wanted Andrew to object. Kelly picked up on this and rapidly grabbed Andrew's hand and requested that he left it alone.

"Just get me a pint," Andrew said in a dismissive manner. "And a white wine, oh and we'll have meatballs with pasta and a calzone for our mains."

The waiter left and Kelly gave her husband a little nod and a squeeze of the hand to let him know he handled it well. The conversation soon came to the biggest achievement they shared, their daughter. Known by her family for her kind nature and warm heart she was given the nickname, 'Sweetie'.

Like the toffee from a toffee apple to skin, she stuck her parents together when they were drifting apart. Similar to the core of a toffee apple, she made her father feel complete, the apple in Andrew's eye. She would help anyone facing hard times, putting her troubles aside, as if she did not matter. Pretty, polite, and full of passion, she had a glow that could not be truly captured by a camera lens.

During the conversation, Andrew noticed his wife continually looking at the waiter who had been rude to him, it was making him furious. Even talk of their precious daughter could not help stop what was about to come.

"What the hell is your problem, why do you keep staring at him?" snarled Andrew.

Kelly was taken aback, not by the tone, or the way she was spoken to, but because of the face he pulled while saying it. Eyes bulging, popping out of his head. His teeth showing, snarling, making every word clear. Face scrunched like a paper bag and a vein pulsating like a banging drum out of the side of his forehead. He looked evil; Kelly knew that look all too well.

"N-N-Nothing, I'm not," replied Kelly sheepishly, while looking at her empty plate.

"Yes, you were, do not lie to me you dirty cow," shouted Andrew, attracting the attention of other diners.

Kelly's head dropped like a sack of potatoes from the shame. This reaction fuelled Andrew's response further: "Go on admit it, you think you can do better than me. Well, you can't, because you are absolutely useless."

By this time, all of the little Italian restaurant's customers and staff could do nothing but gasp in horror. The atmosphere changed from being relaxed and laid back, to tense and on edge. The waiter picked up on the atmosphere and rapidly approached the couple's table to try and resolve the issue.

As the waiter approached the table, Andrew saw him out of the corner of his eye and made a snide remark to Kelly.

"Your knight in shining armour is here. He has come to your rescue, look."

Kelly turned her head slightly to her left, and to no surprise, the waiter was there. The waiter paid no attention to Andrew and asked her if she was okay. Kelly acted like she did not hear him.

"Madam, are you okay?" the waiter asked, putting his hand on her shoulder.

As the waiter's hand touched Kelly, she felt safe and wanted to burst into tears like a river bursting its bank and scream out, 'NO! NO! It is not okay'.

But before Kelly could speak, Andrew projected from his seat like a rocket and yelled, "Get your dirty hands off my wife".

He pushed the waiter into two of his colleagues that came to assist. Standing up and straightening his clothes, the waiter and his colleagues politely but firmly asked Andrew to leave.

It was only a few seconds, but it felt like a lifetime. The entire restaurant was quiet, in a total sense of suspense you could hear the adrenaline pumping around Andrew's body. The silence was broken by the sound of falling drinks and cutlery as Andrew nudged the table lunging towards the waiter with his fists clenched. Before he could make contact, the three waiters tackled him to the ground like they were playing rugby. The waiters escorted him out of the restaurant as the diners cheered.

Andrew's level of aggression accelerated as if his pedal was pressed to the metal. With waiters holding his hands behind his back, Andrew used all his force to kick the glass door open; a true spartan kick. As the sole of his shoes connected with the door, there was a dull vibration that shook through his leg and paused at his hip before stopping. The door's well-oiled hinges allowed it to move backwards like a swing. However, it did not swing back. When fully extended, the door shattered into a thousand little pieces of glass. The chunks of glass collided with the floor like scattering marbles. The pieces of glass covered the floor like stars in the night sky, glistening.

Crunching over the glass as if it were snow, Andrew promptly ran off. Kelly did not know whether she should chase after her husband or stay to help clean up. She wished she could be ripped in half like a piece of paper to make both sides happy but that was not an option. Sincerely apologising for the mess and promising she would come back to square any debts; Kelly ran after her husband.

"Andrew, Andrew. What is wrong? Wait for me. Please don't leave me," Kelly screamed, in an attempt to get Andrew's attention.

She had no money, it was dark, and she was scared. She had no option but to chase after him.

THREE

THE KNIGHT IN SHINING AMOUR

Sean placed his headphones on his head and walked into the town centre to catch the bus. He took each step in time with the beat, boom, boom, boom and skipping any song with a slow tempo to eliminate the risk of delay.

The bitterness of the night's air-kissed his cheeks as a gentle reminder that any body part exposed would succumb to the same fate. The soft leather padding of the headphones cupped his ears like hands, keeping them warm and safe, preventing them from exposure. In sequence, his head nodded like a Churchill dog as the soles of his new trainers graced the dirty floor. Beep. Silence. His head came to a standstill and his pace decreased until he stopped.

He received a notification on his phone. As soon as his hand left his pocket to retrieve his phone to check, the night's air gave his hand a kiss. Sending a shiver up his arm and down his back like a ripple. Buurrr! The notification was Hannah, saying she could not wait to go for some food after the party. The message ended with an emoji blowing a kiss, making Sean smile so big his ears connected. With his music back on, Sean put his hands back into his warm pockets, and continued to walk to his destination, upping his pace.

As Andrew eluded the restaurant staff, he became engulfed with rage. The cold air connected with his warm body to cool him down. The two elements danced together: The cold, in an ice blue suit, with identical ice blue shoes and tie. The warmth, in a red-hot dress and red-hot shoes, leaving a trail of flames after every step. Andrew could not be cooled, nor calmed, his problems were not under control, they needed to be tamed. Steaming up the road like a locomotive, he came to a screeching halt, taking a sharp right after noticing a gap between two buildings.

While strolling up the alley, he reached into his back pocket to get his wallet. Opening it, before finding cover behind an industrial bin the size of a van. Andrew frantically searched through his wallet for the white substance, but to no avail, his heart sinking and his chest becoming heavy as if he were wearing a gold chain that could be used to secure a motorbike.

Bang, Andrew kicked the bin and cursed. In a desperate attempt to tame his demons, he pulled out his red bank card and used the tip of his tongue to run across its edge, absorbing the residue. Andrew let out the biggest 'Arrrgrhhhh', using every particle of air in his lungs. Again, striking the bin with his foot. However, this time he left a dent. The deep thud echoed down the alley disturbing the silent rats. Andrew scurried from the alley like the rats from behind the bin. He pulled his phone from his pocket to make a call and proceeded to walk into the town centre.

Kelly recognised a silhouette in the distance, screaming to gain his attention. The distant shadow vanishing before her, as if her calls were not meant for it. She frantically rushed to try and catch up. Her tears trickled vertically as she ran against the wind: leaving a black trace of mascara. With her lips trembling, Kelly hugged her bag like a teddy bear: mostly to keep warm and partly to feel some form of comfort.

Noticing that people were looking at her in an odd manner, she tried to settle her emotions with nothing but a blubber and a teary outburst every now and again. Just as she turned on to the high street, her husband was there. With all her might, she let out one last call for her husband, which caught his attention. Catching up with him outside of the bank, Kelly blubbered while wiping her tears away.

"Andrew what is wrong with you, we need to go home."

Just as she stopped in front of Andrew, he turned around and struck Kelly across the face with the back of his hand. Kelly flew back towards the wall, hitting her back on the corner.

"Go back to your new boyfriend, you slag," Andrew said angrily, while a white foam dribbled from his mouth like a dog with rabies.

He clenched his right fist and threw it towards Kelly's stomach, striking all of the air out of her body. She made a sound that was not quite a word, as the air left her lungs, and slid to the ground. Kelly, with her hand comforting the blow, used the wall to get back up to her feet.

Andrew did not help, he just stood over her and hurled abuse, like his tongue was a baseball machine spitting out balls. Kelly was petrified, she did not have the courage to answer back. Enraging him further, he pulled his leg back ready to strike Kelly in her face as if her head was a football. As Andrew was about to release his leg, he was tackled to the ground from behind.

It was Sean, he saw what was happening from down the road and ran straight over. He couldn't help notice the fact that other people were walking past, without batting an eyelid as if it were normal for a man to treat a woman like that.

After tackling Andrew to the ground, Sean asked him what he was playing at, pointing out the fact he could have killed her. Andrew showed no remorse or sympathy while getting to his feet. Andrew swung at Sean with enough power to take his head off his shoulders. The fact that he protracted the punch as he was trying to get so much power, made it easy for Sean to see.

Ducking under the swing, Sean said, "What are you doing yo, don't make me hurt you old man."

It made no difference. Andrew saw Sean as a red flag and charged at him like a bull with all his might. Grabbing Sean around the waist, Andrew pushed Sean backwards into the wall. Sean's head bounced off the wall like a bouncy ball causing him to lose consciousness momentarily. Sean elbowed Andrew in the middle of his back so he instantly let go, allowing him to break free. Sean's sight focused, the noise of the passing traffic in the background was eliminated, and his heart was pounding.

Sean was in fight mode. He raised his fists up to his chin and took on a boxing stance. Andrew attacked again. However, this time before Andrew could grab Sean, Andrew's red cheek was met with Sean's rock-solid fist. Crack! The impact caused a ripple on Andrew's face, switching off the signals to his brain, leaving him in an unconscious heap on the floor.

Sean shouted, "See, I told you that would happen yo."

Andrew laid unresponsive. Sean's attention was turned to Kelly who had slid back down and was now using the wall as an aid to get up.

"Woah, woah, watch it babe," he said. You're hurt, let me help you."

He took her hand, gently pulling her up from the ground. Kelly thanked him for what he did but in a dismissive way. Although, she would have preferred it if he had just left her alone.

Sean noticed her tone but did not want her to go through any more pain, so he insisted on trying to persuade Kelly to call the police. She would not, because she could not ensure that the police could keep her safe in the long run. Sean could see the worry on her face and realised the police were not an option, so he offered to escort her to find a taxi. Just as they turned, the street light shone on her face, and he realised that he recognised her.

He turned to her, "Wait, aren't you -"

Sean could not finish his sentence, he felt three blows: two on his back near his shoulder blade and the final one at the side of his neck.

Kelly screamed so loud, it echoed through the streets. At first, Sean thought he had been punched by Andrew, but the terror and shock on Kelly's face told him otherwise. Sean grabbed his neck as the blow left it feeling heavy. His palms touched his neck and felt wet. He moved his hand round to see what was causing the sensation.

"Blood!" Sean heard Kelly yell in despair. "You've stabbed him, you've..."

Sean's hearing became muffled. His vision was blurry and got darker, until there was nothing but darkness.

He lay there lifeless. Kelly tried her best to comfort the young boy but against all her desperate attempts, she was overpowered and dragged away by her husband. Like an echo, her cries got quieter as she was dragged further away. Meanwhile concerned bystanders flocked around Sean, as if they were blocking him from evil spirits trying to collect his soul.

One person spoke to the emergency services, passing on instructions. "Right, you need to apply pressure to the wound."

"Has anyone got a cloth?" the male on the ground demanded urgently.

A woman unwrapped her scarf and passed it to the man knelt beside Sean. He applied pressure to the neck. The blood continued to trickle on to the street as if it were a drunk person trying to walk straight.

"How is he still bleeding? said one of them.

A moment of silence unified all of those around the body. They removed his coat and jumper revealing his blood-soaked T-shirt.

"There on his back."

His jumper was scrunched up like a piece of paper and pressed against the wounds on his back.

"C'mon kid. Stay with me. Everything will be okay," the good Samaritan said, while applying pressure.

Chuf. Chuf. Chuf. The blades sliced through the air like a sword through a watermelon. Chuf. Chuf. Chuf. The propeller spinning like a drum in a washing machine. A light shone down on the group, making it hard for them to see. Shading their eyes from the light, the machine became visible. The air ambulance had arrived. The pilot was in full control of the machine, hovering slowly to allow it to land safely within the car-free area of the road, as if he were simply putting a drink down on a coaster.

Two paramedics leapt out of the helicopter and sprinted, with bags in hand towards the scene.

"Clear the area, we need space to work," the first paramedic said assertively. The crowd parted as did the ocean for Moses.

Sean slipped back into consciousness. He heard, "Hello, can you hear me?"

As one paramedic was asking for information, the other took a pair of scissors out of their bag and cut Sean's t-shirt off as if they were cutting through wrapping paper.

"We're the paramedics, here to take you to the..."

He let out a grunt before slipping back into his unconscious state. The burgundy of the blood overlapped the white of his t-shirt as if it were the tide coming in over the sand. Both paramedics praised the group of people for locating the stab wounds and slowing the bleeding.

Continuing to keep pressure on the wounds, the paramedics wrapped Sean's body in a silver foil blanket, like a savoury snack in tin foil. He was rolled on to a stretcher, then lifted onto to the wheels and pushed away.

The good Samaritans with their blood-soaked hands and teary eyes shared a moment of spiritual harmony. No words. No movement. Just a sense of togetherness. Resulting in the group hugging each other before having their statements taken along with their contact details. They said their goodbyes and carried on with life, hoping that they had done enough.

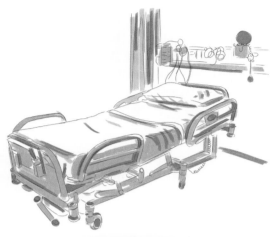

FOUR

IN SAFE HANDS

The two wounds on Sean's back were addressed before the helicopter was airborne. Allowing for the paramedic's attention to be brought to the wound on his neck, which was still trickling blood. Nerves got the better of one of the paramedics as he desperately foraged through drawers to find the correct medical equipment. While the other paramedic got the apparatus to take Sean's observations. Although the helicopter was as big as a minibus, there was not much room for inside the paramedics to move.

Sean's arm was guided through the hoop of the blood pressure cuff, stopping midway up his bicep. The churn of the machine pushed air into the device causing it to inflate. When at the correct pressure it stopped, looking like a swimming armband. Beep. Beep. Beep. The machine sounded in harmony with his heartbeat: he had a pulse.

"Come on kid, hang in there for me," said the paramedic, while clipping an oximeter to Sean's finger like a clothing peg.

With the bleeding almost under control, the paramedics made a call to the trauma team in the accident and emergency unit of the local hospital. The paramedic picked up the bulky phone and punched in the number to ensure it was entered correctly.

"We have a young male between sixteen and twenty-four. Three puncture wounds, two on his back located near the scapula and one further puncture at the bottom of his neck, heading down past the collarbone. The bleeding of the two near the shoulder blade is under control. However, the bleeding from the wound on the neck is not stable. He has lost a lot of blood; observations are reading around 28%. We will be with you in three minutes."

The nurse slammed the phone down with a crash without saying goodbye and did a call out.

"Air ambulance is three minutes away. I need a theatre ready, anaesthetist, surgeon and three support staff on me, now!"

The nurse grabbed the crash trolly and headed to the entrance to meet the helicopter. Sensing the urgency in the nurse's voice, the requested staff were hot on her heels. The floor screeching as the rubber on the soles of their shoes came to a sudden halt as they reached the entrance. The nurse gave the staff a quick brief as they anxiously waited.

"It sounds like we could be dealing with a Class 3 Haemorrhage. This young man has very low blood pressure and a high heart rate. Two wounds on the back near the shoulder blade and another on his neck. Let's hope he is a fighter."

The air ambulance steadied before it landed on the helipad, like a dragonfly on a lily pad. Without giving the propeller a chance to stop spinning, the trauma team were waiting at the door of the big bird. The heavy door of the helicopter made a deep grinding noise, shaking the aluminium frame on the crash trolley as it opened. The motionless body met the trauma team, time slowed down. The inside looked like a horror film, blood everywhere. Up the walls and blood-soaked bandages in the middle of puddles of blood covering the floor. It looked like a tin of red paint had been thrown inside.

The nurse felt a lump in her throat and swallowed hard but no luck. She stepped into the helicopter to pull the body out and noticed one paramedic sitting on the floor with his head in his hands, using his knees to support his elbows. Her eyes met with the other paramedics as she twisted around to reach out for the crash mat. The nurse followed the paramedic's eyes to the body and back.

The paramedic then dropped her head, both had clearly been through a traumatic experience. Beep, Beep, Beep. The rhythm of the machine's noise caught the nurse's attention.

Focused again she yelled, "Right, come on team, let's get this young man the help he needs".

As they slid his body from the helicopter, his neck wound started spitting blood over the trauma team. A support worker grabbed a blood sample tub, while another reapplied pressure to the wound. He filled the tub with blood and sprinted towards the hospital like a runner to the finishing line. He knew time was not on their side, Sean needed blood and fast.

The anxiety of the team was quickly overtaken by adrenalin, rapidly getting Sean to the operating theatre. Before Sean's body was hooked up to the machines, it started convulsing, then suddenly stopped. The surgeon's trained eye noticed a lack of movement in his chest: he had stopped breathing.

A support worker saw the panic in the surgeon's face and grabbed Sean's wrist to which she found no pulse.

"He's gone into shock, quick get the defibrillator," the surgeon instructed.

The defibrillator was no bigger than a lunch box, with two wires leading to two pads, which could have been mistaken for travel irons. The box made a high-pitched screech while charging, the light turned green.

"CLEAR."

The surgeon applied the pads to Sean's chest. THUD, THUD. Sean's body jumped. No change. No pulse. No breath. The surgeon lifted the pads until the light returned to green.

"CLEAR".

THUD, THUD. Sean's body jumped, but again. No change. No pulse. No breath.

"CLEAR". THUD, THUD.

The support worker yelled, "There's a pulse."

The surgeon threw the pad from his right hand, sending it sliding across the shiny surface of the metal counter. He then put the back of his hand to Sean's mouth, dropping his head and squinting his eyes, concentrating on any feeling that may occur. The surgeon's heartbeat slowed down as he concentrated, all of his senses focusing on the small area on the back of his hand. Suddenly, the hairs on the back of his hand swayed, then stopped and swayed again. He was breathing.

"Well done team, he's back. We've got a long way to go but he's back." The surgeon panted in relief.

The nurse came in with three pints of blood and administered it. They all left the room, leaving Sean hooked up to the monitoring devices and the life support machine. Beep. Beep. Beep. The light in the operating theatre dimmed as there was no other movement. Sean was illuminated by nothing but the reflection of the bright display from the equipment. Heart pumping. Blood flowing. Breathing because of a machine.

The trauma team left and regrouped in the staff room. All visibly tired, with bags under their eyes, big enough to carry the emotional stress their day had entailed. Covered in the blood, sweat, and tears. A sense of uncertainty was lurking, doubt prevented the team from looking each other in the eye.

The surgeon broke the silence. "C'mon people, heads up. The bleeding has stopped, but he lost a lot of blood. His body is accepting the blood transfusion. His heart is beating but we do not yet know the true extent of the damage to his body. Do we have a name for the young man? We really need to inform his next-of-kin."

While wiping a tear from his eye, a member of the support staff volunteered to complete the task at hand. Partly to help, but for the most part, to leave the tense atmosphere of the room. The support worker used Sean's bus pass to retrieve his identity and search for his details to locate his next of kin, his mother. The police were called so they could collect his mother and bring her to the hospital.

FIVE

A MOTHERS HORROR TO HEAR

The police officer took a deep breath as he extended his arm, looking towards his colleague for support. The hair on his wrist stood up as the cold touched his exposed skin, his hand hovered in front of the door like a hummingbird. With the nod of support from his colleague, the officer knocked on the door. Boom. Boom. Boom.

Slumped in her chair in the front room, Sean's mother Charlotte had slipped into a deep sleep after watching her favourite soap. An activity that became regular since she had undertaken her second job. The sound from the door was like thunder, leaving a tense feeling within the room like it was going to rain. Charlotte almost jumped out of her skin, grabbing the arms of her chair as she rocketed upright. Eyes as wide as a panoramic view and heart beating like a drum, she took a moment to gather her bearings.

A second barrage of knocks struck the door. Charlotte curiously picked up the remote and pressed mute: silence. In a state of shock her heartbeat slowed, allowing her to listen for any movement at the front door in between her heart beats. She heard talking, with a puzzled look she went to the door to see who it was.

Approaching the dark PVC front door, two people could be made out through the two panels of frosted glass. Both wearing black hats, pointed like the end of a bullet and dark clothes merging into the night sky. Charlotte approached the door anxiously, her hand following the wall's smooth but grainy texture. She had no clue as to their age, race, gender, or purpose. As she crept towards her door, a small green light stole her attention. It looked like a glow-worm in the night. With one eyebrow raised, a radio, she whispered to herself.

"Hello, Ms Barkly. Are you there? It is the police," said the officer from outside.

Charlotte gasped and she hurried down the hallway. The soft grainy texture of the wall now felt like sandpaper on her fingertips as she rushed to the door.

With her mind full of fear and a mix of emotions controlling her voice box, she roared, "WHAT DO YOU WANT?"

Taken aback, the police officer replied, "There has been an incident with your son, Sean. Could you come with us, please?"

When Charlotte heard the officer say 'incident', her fear quickly turned into worry, coursing through her blood like poison. The second she heard her son's name, the life drained from her body. Her body as weak as a frail old lady, she knew what was coming but was not ready for the blow. Shaking, Charlotte desperately attempted to unlock the door to talk to the officers, but she was only able to rattle the bunch of keys.

"Ms Barkly, just take some deep breaths and try again. We'll wait."

Her hearing muffled and vision blurred; the advice was missed. By chance, Charlotte was able to unlock the door. Before the door was fully ajar, she fired questions at the officer as she burst into tears. The officer engaging with Charlotte was only able to make out her asking if Sean was okay.

"He is in the best place, we -"

"Look, we do not have time for this," the second officer abruptly interrupted. "You need to collect your belongings and come with us to the hospital."

The stern voice of the officer shocked Charlotte back into reality. As she wiped away her tears, she dashed back through the hallway into the front room and grabbed her black leather handbag.

After locking the door, she followed the police officers to their patrol vehicle. Once in the privacy of the car, the officer turned to Charlotte and explained that her son had been involved in an altercation and was the victim of a stabbing.

"My son was stabbed? Who would want to stab Sean, he is the most caring and respectful boy? Are you sure it is my son?" Charlotte questioned.

The officer confirmed it was Sean as they had his ID. "Our inspectors are looking into what happened as we speak. Currently, all we know is that the assault happened near the town centre."

A smile of sympathy ended the conversation. The image of Sean laying there, in so much pain punctured the forefront of her thoughts.

"My son, who would do such a terrible act on my gentle, loving Sean."

Charlotte could not understand. Trying to piece together the night's events, she phoned Kiki hoping to gain more information, but there was no answer. Staring out of the car window, Charlotte was lost. The rain trickled down the window, mirroring the tears trickling down her face. All the streetlights appeared as one long light, like a sparkler on bonfire night.

Every so often, Charlotte would see a building she recognised when the blue light of the police car illuminated its surroundings. She had travelled these roads hundreds of times, but never in her current state of mind. Her mind occupied with images of her son, vulnerable, helpless, in pain. Minutes felt like hours, one mile felt like ten, when a son needs his mother the most.

Arriving at the hospital, the police officer pushed his foot on the break, forcing all the participants to jolt forward, Charlotte snapped out of her trance-like state. She could feel her son was close. Pulling on the chrome door handle, she used her shoulder to open the car door. The door did not open, she pushed against the door with her shoulder again. Thud! No effect. Charlotte's anxiety spiked rapidly. Her heart rate doubled. Her breath halved.

In a state of panic, she pulled the handle and banged her shoulder against the door frantically screaming, "MY SON, MY SON, LET ME SEE MY SON!"

Thud. Thud. Thud. The police officer opened the door from the outside. Charlotte tumbled out of the police car. Jumping to her feet and running, she busted through the entrance of accident and emergency department doors like a bat out of hell. Putting two and two together, she thought her son would be on this ward.

As she yanked off the curtains to the bays searching for her son, Charlotte screamed, "Sean, where are you? I'm here. Mummy is here for you!"

The shocked faces of patients greeted her. A nurse heard the commotion and rushed over to investigate before more patients were disturbed. Charlotte caught the nurse approaching out of the corner of her eye, she pivoted and made a beeline for her, pleading for help find her son. The nurse knew where Sean was, as it was the only room in the hospital with armed guards. Catching Charlotte in her arms, she escorted her through the hospital to Sean.

Standing at around six foot two inches tall, with a combined weight of a car, two hard faced police officers blocked the door. One hand on the trigger and the other holding the

base of their black submachine guns. Whatever was behind the doors needed to be kept
safe.

As Charlotte got closer to the door, she could
feel her son was behind it. She broke away
from the nurse's comforting hold and made a
run for the door with so much speed, her hair
blew out of her face. Just as she was about to
push open the door, she was lifted from the
floor. Her legs were still moving, but she was
not moving forward. The police officers had
lifted her from the floor to prevent her from
entering.

Trying to wriggle her way back to the ground
she yelled, "My son, my son is in there". The
door opened; it was the surgeon. While propping the door open, she requested the officers
let Charlotte go.

"Come in Ms Barkly, Sean has been waiting for
you."

The pain from the gut-wrenching feeling in the
pit of Charlotte's stomach caused her to cry.
Her tears washed away any hope of the person
laying there not being her beloved son.

She rushed over and gently resting her head
against his, whispered, "I'm here for you my
love, don't worry."

Holding his hand, she gently kissed his head before asking the surgeon if he was going to be okay. The surgeon then went on to explain that Sean had lost a lot of blood from three stab wounds. Staff had done an excellent job to stabilise him, but the machine was now breathing for him.

Charlotte leant back on the chair and looked at her son. The tube sticking out of his mouth was keeping him alive. The wires attached to his fingertips made him look like an octopus with extended tentacles tracking his health.

"Please Son, stay strong you will get through this." Charlotte sobbed.

SIX

MUM KNOWS BEST

The tears dropped from Charlotte's pale face, like a tap that was not quite turned off. As the tears collided with the floor, one droplet turned into ten smaller droplets resting in a puddle. Budging her chair as close to Sean as it would allow her, each movement produced a screeching sound as the chair legs scraped across the floor. Charlotte clutched her son's hand and began to speak.

"I remember the day you were born like it was yesterday. You were so different, as soon as your tiny lungs were filled with air you smiled. Unlike your big brother who cried the whole hospital down. Your smile did not stop there;

from the moment you had your food to the moment you went to sleep, you were such a happy baby."

Charlotte looked down at her son's hand and began to stroke it. "The way your hair only grew around the sides like an old man and your laugh: your laugh came from your belly. It would have me laughing with you for hours on end. 'Bro' was your first ever word, Michael absolutely loved that."

The thought made her smile. "When we picked him up from school, he would bring all friends round to show you off. But before he could even get near the pram, you would shout, 'Bro, Bro, Bro'. Michael would turn to all of his friends and say, 'I told you he could sense me before he saw me. He has definitely got super-powers'. All his friends would agree and ask for you to shout them. You loved having a big brother.

I haven't talked too much about Michael as I didn't want his lifestyle choices to rub off on you. I don't know the ins and outs of it myself, but I will tell you what I do know. Michael took on the role of the man of the house when your father left. A huge role for an eighteen-year-old. We were such a strong family unit; he would go out to work at the local car parts centre and come home with us.

We didn't have a lot of money but we got by. Until things went horribly wrong when Michael got himself into an argument with a local drug dealer. Capo and his runners used to sell drugs at the entrance of the flats. It was always full of drug addicts, the smell of drugs was so bad, and they often bullied people as they passed. I think what really wound your brother up was that families used the entrance.

The argument did not sit well with Capo as he felt Michael was trying to show him up, but rather than assaulting Michael, Capo went one step further and attempted to humiliate your brother. Capo noticed that your brother was always in his Euro bits uniform, and that in fact, one of Capo's clients was the manager there. So, Capo enticed the manager with free drugs and the two set Michael up to lose his job. It worked, they planted items in Michael's bag, so it looked as if he had stolen them. Your brother was devastated when he lost his job, he felt as if he had failed us.

As days turned into weeks, Michael stopped speaking to his friends, he stopped playing with you and he became very difficult to talk to. He would lock himself in his room on his laptop for days on end. I was able to talk Michael into signing on to bring some money in. This is something neither of us wanted as we did not want to rely on the state to provide for us, but what else could we do? I didn't want us to be a family on benefits, I wanted you guys to be raised with my hard-working attitude. But we were struggling, struggling bad.

My worries about your brother grew, he began to leave the house in the early hours of the morning. He was becoming secretive and began hiding things. I thought he was selling drugs. I confronted him. Like an unhappy puppy, I could see the disappointment in his eyes when I asked him. He was so upset that I thought he would do such a thing. But there was nothing else that could explain his actions.

Confronting him on his behaviour was bittersweet. I hoped he was not selling drugs or involved in a gang, but I couldn't put my finger on what it was. So, I waited up one morning and looked on his laptop for what it might be. I watched a YouTube video on how to find the search history. I could not believe what I found: Juju. Black magic. Rituals. Spiritual powers. At first, I thought it was some religious cult that was attempting to groom Michael into illegalities. But it wasn't. Michael was trying to get help spiritually to help deal with our current situation. I wasn't unhappy or happy with it as I didn't know much about it, but it was helping him cope. He began to come back out of his shell. The old, loving, funny Michael was coming back to us.

One day you were ill at nursery, I tried to get through to your brother but failed. So I finished work early, collected you, and took you straight home. I opened the door to the living room; I was taken aback with what I saw. The room was dark, the only light came from candles placed in a circle on the floor. The flickering flames illuminated something on the floor, at first inspection I thought it was a bundle of dirty washing. As the light flickered, I looked closer. It was a chicken, a dead chicken. I traced the trickles of blood across a blanket to the wall.

There was a picture on the wall. It wasn't drawn, it was smeared with the blood of the animal carcass. I couldn't get a good enough look, so I took a step into the room when a voice roared from the corner, 'Get out'. It made me jump, I put my hand over my heart to stop it from beating out of my chest. Michael stepped out of the darkness, his face looked like a skull, his eyes and nose painted black and the rest of his face was painted white. His mouth and bare chest were covered in dried blood, like he had drank it. His eyes were as white as snow. His voice sounded deeper than normal. It was like he was possessed. Before I had the chance to say anything, he roared again, 'Now'. I was so scared, that thing there looked like your brother, but it was not him. Whatever it was, it was pure evil.

We left as fast as possible. A few days later, I got a call from Michael saying we were able to go back home. I tried to ask him what was going on, but he assured me everything was okay, and we should go back. That night, Michael told me he was practising witchcraft to allow his spirits to make good fortune for him. The chants were calls to the Gods, and the chicken was his sacrifice for good fortune. I really did not know what to do, but it seemed to work for Michael, so I felt I had to be alright with it. The conversation ended with me telling him how I felt, there were tears and hugs. That was the last time I hugged my eldest son. The pressure of him not being able to provide for us, him not being able to get a new job and Capo's continuous aggravation got to him, like a piece of dry spaghetti. He snapped.

One evening, I saw Michael coming back from shopping. Capo and his friends were crowding the doorway. He pushed his way through the bodies and despite the taunts, he kept his head down. Until, Capo struck the shopping bag with his foot. The thin plastic bag tore, shopping came tumbling out of the split and covered the cold floor. Michael told me how the built-up anger rushed through his body, feeling like he was on fire. He turned to Capo and hit him with his head, the connection was like a hammer hitting a nail. SPLAT!

Capo's nose broke, upon impact, blood splatting on those within a close enough proximity. The impact forced him to the floor. His allies could see the evil in Michael's eyes and stepped back. Holding his nose, Capo attempted to get to his feet. Before he could plant them on the ground, Michael pounced on him like a lion. With his knees over Capo's waist, Michael raised his fist to strike Capo, but he didn't. He wanted to humiliate Capo, like he had done to him.

Michael picked up a tin of beans, while Capo kicked his legs, trying to defend himself. Michael looked at the tin then proceeded to pound Capo's head until he lost consciousness. Covered in blood, Michael got up from the floor and patted down Capo's pockets, taking his money, phone, and drugs.

Glaring at Capo's associates, Michael went around every one of them and looked them in the eye and said, 'You lot work for me now, if you have a problem with that say sutten'.

The hustle and bustle of the crowd went silent, nobody dared move, or look back in your brother's direction. He ordered them to leave and never to do anything in that stairwell again.

From that day, your brother controlled the estate. As weeks went on, Michael came around less and less, he got so wrapped up in that lifestyle. He stopped bringing the money around himself, he got one of the young kids to do it. I was worried that he would get hurt, I tried to talk to him, but he always said he would be fine. I was hearing stories of him hurting people bad - families and their friends. They started to call him Big Juj, I knew that this was because of him practising Juju. The rumour was that he had started killing people that crossed him, calling them his sacrifices. This was not the son I had brought up. The streets had a hold of him, and I was not going to risk that with you. So, we left. I hope you understand why I hid this from you."

Charlotte's attention returned to her circumstances. She was still none the wiser as to what had happened to her youngest son. Deep in thought, Charlotte had almost dozed off in the chair when her phone began to ring. Blurry eyed, she answered, it was Kiki. She questioned her as to what happened, she did not know. Kiki wanted to come to the hospital, but Charlotte declined until she had figured out what had happened. She would have stayed awake if she possibly could, but her eyelids became too heavy and consequently won the fight.

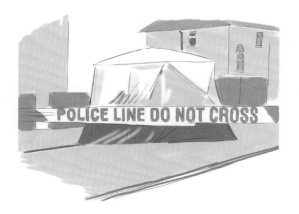

SEVEN

PIECING THE PUZZLE

Detective Chief Inspector (DCI) Summers looked at her reflection in the rear-view mirror, noticing the white hairs coming through, she scraped the stray hairs back into her hairband. Her attention was then drawn to the bags under her eyes. Pulling on her skin, she tried to see what she would look like if she could ever relax. She sighed. *A life with no stress*, she muttered, while opening the car door.

Summers did not get enough time to put on her usual work attire of heels, fitted pencil skirt, white shirt, and black blazer. Instead she wore a blue water-resistant coat, zipped all the way up, covering her creased t-shirt and a pair of light blue jeans that she'd had on earlier in the day to walk her dog.

Approaching the taped crime scene, she spotted a white forensics tent on one side of the path, and on the other side was a few yellow markers with numbers on them. The section in between the two points looked like it used to be a road. But as the town centre was so busy it had been blocked off to cars to make more room for shoppers.

Her years of experience enabled her to make a mental checklist of what she saw and put together different scenarios. Her game was to work out what had happened before speaking to anyone about the incident.

The white forensic tent was up, it was bad, possibly a death. The size of the taped off area was large, so the incident must have lasted for quite a long time. There was no blood between the two points, which meant there were two parts to the incident. The high street was covered in cameras and extremely busy. So, whoever did this would be getting paid a visit shortly.

It was now Detective Summers' time to shine, she ducked under the police tape like ropes into a boxing ring. Ready. Determined. Focused.

"Good evening Ma'am, it's a pleasure to see you," said the officer in charge of the crime scene.

A thorough update was then given to her: there has been a stabbing, a young male, seventeen-years-old.

"We have completed concurrent witness statements, eleven in total. All identical. There was an assault on a middle-aged woman by a middle-aged man. The young man stepped in just before the older male kicked the woman in her face. The young male warned the older male to stay away. The man ignored the warning, which resulted in the young male striking the older male to the ground. While the young male turned his attention to the battered woman, the older male stabbed him from behind. The woman tried to help the young boy, but she was dragged away. They absconded down the road."

"Right," said Summer. "First things first, we need to find out who this man and woman are. Look over the CCTV and see where they went and how they got there."

As Summers pulled back the makeshift door of the forensic tent, the metallic and slightly sweet smell of blood hit her nose like a speeding train. She quickly pulled up the collar of her coat, to block the smell. A large puddle of blood was the centrepiece of the tent. The temporary lights reflecting from it, like the sunset on a river. This was certainly not the first bloody crime scene she had been to, nor was it the bloodiest. But by far, that was the largest pool of blood she had ever seen. Her instincts taught her it was not looking good for the victim.

She observed people in white suits crouching down, examining the ground. She noticed pieces of glass shimmering as the light bounced off its surface. The first thought was that the weapon was a piece of glass. She knelt down and put white rubber gloves on with a slap on the wrist. Summers picked up a piece of glass between her thumb and index finger. As she brought it closer to her view, she closed one eye to get a better look. There were no remnants of blood, and the glass was thick. Thicker than a glass bottle or a normal window.

Her mind led her to a bus shelter: when she was younger, she remembered being told off for playing too close to broken glass at a bus stop, where the glass on the shelter was shattered.

Ruling out glass as the weapon, her mind tried to find a reason for bits of glass. A light bulb moment, there might have been a smashed industrial-sized window, or a glass door related to this incident.

Summers exited the tent to look for any smashed doors or windows, in close proximity. None. However, her eagle eye spotted a trail of glass down the road. Ducking under the tape she hoped her instinct was correct. Hot on the tail of a clue, she felt victorious until the trail came to an abrupt end down an alley, crushing her confidence.

"Damn," she yelled in frustration. She had hit a brick wall and so used this time to get an update on the CCTV.

The DCI called the CCTV operation control room.

Ear to phone, "Ma'am, we have found the incident on camera, it matches statements made by the witnesses. We've tracked the couple heading north and fleeing in a silver private taxi. We have the plates; we are running them through our resources to find where they were dropped off. It may take a little longer than normal as it was not a pre-booked taxi. A clear picture of both suspects will be with you any moment. Oh, one more thing ma'am, the knife. The CCTV shows that it was the victim's knife that fell out during the tussle and the attacker picked it up. Just to clarify, the victim did not or attempt to pull out the knife".

Summers added to her mental notes. *This was definitely not a targeted attack, looks to be fuelled by alcohol maybe.*

She told the officer the progress she had made and requested he look on the system for any reports of criminal damage or violence in the area, two hours prior to the incident and ended the phone call. Puzzled, there was only one way to go.

Coming out of the alley, she continued to walk down the main road. It amazed Summers how something so devastating could happen so close, yet nobody knew. Tap. Tap. Tap. The sound brought Summers out of her thoughts. It sounded like she had heels on, but only on one foot. She dragged her foot against the floor to try and rid the noise. Her foot scraped along the ground, leaving a white mark. Propping herself up against a wall, inspected the sole of her shoe. Glass. She must be close.

The hustle and bustle of the nightlife masked the sound of the workmen fixing a broken door several units down. A few seconds later, Summers was standing outside the Italian restaurant, as if fate had brought them together. Entering the restaurant, Summers introduced herself and asked the waiter for a member of management. The manager came out of the back, hands raised high and waving about, with a frown fixed on his face.

Sternly saying, "It is about time you got here, what am I going to do about my door?"

Summers demanded that the manager calmed down and listen. She informed him that she was not there about the door but her case and the incident at the restaurant may be related.

The manager apologised and begged for her to understand his actions. He continued by telling her about the events of the night. As soon as he said a man and woman, she pulled her phone out and placed it in front of the manager.

"This man and woman?" she asked.

"Yes," he said, nodding.

Summers fired questions at the manager. "Did they book a table? What time did they leave? Which direction did they walk off?"

While the manager went in search of members of staff to get the answers, Summers called the office to give an update. During the conversation with headquarters, the manager came back with a name and a home number. Summers made a call to head office to trace the name and number to an address. No sooner had she put down the phone, it vibrated: Kelly Blacks, 32 Rows Road.

The manager returned and answered her questions then added, "That was the man who caused all of the trouble, who terrified my customers with his violent behaviour. I am in fear of that poor woman's life," replied the manager with no hesitation.

"Right, we need an armed response at that location in thirty minutes. DO! NOT! MOVE! until I get there. We need to keep the woman safe," Summers ordered.

Thanking the manager for his help and promising an officer would be in touch, she headed out of the restaurant and darted back to her car.

Arriving at the Black's residence was like something out of a movie. The detached five bedroomed house spread as far as the eye could see. The dark stone had pale fragments, which matched the colour of the drive. The window frames were dark grey, as was the barn house style door. Encased in a huge window, a beautiful chandelier hung between the staircase, like an earring from a model. Lights lit up the path to the extravagant entrance, held up by two colossal columns. A house one could only dream for.

Police officers with guns drawn waited at the front and rear of the property in a semicircle in silence. As if someone had drawn a line around the house with a protractor. Summers signalled for eight officers to follow her. They approached the front door, she pointed to the one with the battering ram to come forward. And then ordered the other officers to enter the property once the door was breached.

Summers knocked hard on the door. "Hello, Mrs Blacks."

Silence. She knocked again. No movement. Summers signalled 3, 2, 1 then pointed at the door. The officer took a deep breath in as he pulled back the battering ram. His cheeks blew up as he exhaled, swinging the ram forward with all his strength at the door. As soon as the ram connected with the door everything began to slow, almost at a standstill.

BOOOOOM! The door flew open, showing no resistance, like it was unlocked. The force from the metal lock split the door frame creating an explosion of splintered wood. Flying through the air like debris in the atmosphere, the splin- tered wood bounced from the officers as they entered the house.

In uniform, the officers shouted, "This is the police, everybody stand still."

Summers spotted a woman sat shaking in a state of despair in a chair. "Female, three o'clock".

Directly ahead was the back door, a figure came dashing into view from the right and made an exit through the back door. The person made it out of the door but just as the door shut, they were tackled to the floor by an officer covering the rear of the property.

With the couple now cuffed in the front room, they were both arrested for attempted murder and read their rights. The woman was screaming dramatically - was it guilt, fear, or shock? With no remorse, the male threatened her to keep her mouth shut. The husband and wife were escorted out of the house to separate police cars. Summers could smell a bully a mile away and Andrew was just that. She stared him in the face until he was driven off. He could not intimidate her, like he could his wife.

With the puzzle somewhat finished, Summers made her way to the hospital to update Charlotte on her findings. Summers' hardened exterior let off no emotion as she saw Sean lay there, lifeless, depending on a machine to keep him alive. Nothing but a shake of the head and a tut.

"Hi, Ms Barkly, I'm DCI Summers. I'm leading the case on the incident with your son. I have come to give you an update on what has happened so far."

Charlotte begged for her to tell her what had happened to her son, she needed answers. Summers told the mother all she knew. Charlotte thought she could not cry any more. She did.

"You mean to tell me. My son is in this state because he defended a woman getting beaten by her husband?"

Summers nodded. "I am afraid to tell you Ms Barkly that CCTV shows that Sean was carrying the knife and dropped it during the incident."

Summers presented Charlotte with an image of the knife and asked if she recognised it.

In total disbelief and horror, Charlotte replied, "Yes, I do, it is one of my kitchen knives".

EIGHT

TRUE COLOURS

Kelly arrived at the local police station first. The entrance was open plan with a desk as soon as you stepped in. Walls magnolia, with dark blue gloss, this was no place for fun. All the windows were frosted with bars on the outside, the lighting emitted from dull strip lights suspended from the ceiling. The walls were full of posters with information. Apart from one which housed nine screens, three up and three across, playing CCTV.

The sergeant at the reception looked up at the clearly shaken Kelly and asked how she was feeling. Her answer could not surface, held down by her heavy heart. She nodded.

"Can you verify your name is Kelly Blacks?" She nodded.

"You are being charged with assisting an offender, a Mr Andrew Blacks."

Her face went as white as a ghost, staring through the officer like he was not sat directly in front of her. She paused for ten seconds before giving another nod.

Kelly was then taken to get a DNA swab and fingerprints taken. The feeling of the cotton bud in her mouth tickled but she could not laugh about her situation, she just pulled her mouth away. Her fingerprints had to be taken a few times as she was shaking so much the machine could not pick them up.

She felt like a criminal, she felt disgusted in herself for being in this predicament. There was nothing but silence as she was escorted to her holding cell. The quiet before the storm.

Not five minutes had passed before the sergeant could hear a commotion outside. He turned to the CCTV to observe what was happening. A male was resisting the officers attempting to bring him in. The sergeant called for two more officers to help restrain him. The additional officers only aggravated the male further. Punching. Kicking. Screaming. The officers had to put him on the floor and bind his legs together. The male was then carried in, with one officer holding each leg and one holding each arm.

The sergeant spun around on his chair to meet them and said, "Mr Blacks, Andrew Blacks I take it."

Andrew could not hear him as he was shouting abuse at the officers. So one of the arresting officers answered on his behalf.

"You are charged with the attempted murder of a Mr Sean Barkly."

That caught Andrew's attention.

"Attempted murder for what, sticking up for myself? Get off me, now. GET OFF NOW!"

Despite being mid-air with no control, Andrew would not calm down.

"I've had enough of this, take him to the cell and leave him cuffed up," said the sergeant. He then picked up the phone and called DCI Summers to inform her that her guests had arrived.

The white brick walls of the holding cell and the thick door between her and the outside world made Kelly feel safe. With nothing but a wooden bed, a steel toilet, and a few splats of blood up the wall to keep her company, Kelly had time to unfold the sequence of events which landed her in a police cell facing jail time.

Sitting on the corner of the bed, she looked down at her hands and wept. Staring at the bloodstains, tears of guilt dropped down her face, bumps in her chin formed as she tried to hold back the feeling of guilt from taking over.

"No. no, no, no, no. What have I done?" she said as she rocked back and forth like a rocking chair. An innocent boy was stabbed and now holding on for his dear life. And all for helping her.

Summers was thirty minutes away. The sergeant updated Kelly and asked if she wanted a solicitor present. Kelly declined, protesting she had nothing to hide. The sergeant then went to check if the interrogation room was ready for DCI Summers' arrival.

Opening the interrogation room brought about an eerie feeling to the sergeant. So many horrific crimes had been admitted to in that room, with no remorse shown in the slightest. The top half padded maroon and the bottom half of the room was painted light grey, the colour white shirts go when they have been washed with something black. Three walls followed suit apart from one, which had a two-way mirror in place of the padding.

In the middle of the room was an old square desk, covered in wood veneer. Woodchip exposed on the more used parts. Four chairs matching the padded decor placed underneath. As if the room had been stuck in time from the 1970s, on the left of the table was a cassette recorder. Open, awaiting to hear a new story. The red button, waiting patiently, ready to capture words that could change the course of someone's life. Next to it sat a stack of cassette tapes.

The unlocking of the mechanism within the door echoed through the cell startling Kelly. She saw the door opening. Blocking the doorway, the sergeant asked Kelly to come through to the interrogation room. Walking through the narrow corridors, reminded her of when she was in school and having to go see the headteacher.

The sergeant did not say a word while walking until he instructed her to enter the correct door. Upon entry, Kelly felt the same eerie feeling course through her body as the sergeant did, from this day on her life would not be the same. Sitting down at the table alone, worried, her future unbeknown. But she was ready. She was ready to make a change.

Moments later, DCI Summers entered the room along with another officer, the usual introductions were made.

"Right Mrs Blacks, I am pressing record now." Click. "May I remind you that you have a right to silence. Whatever you say can be used against you in a criminal case in court. If you don't mention something now which you mention later in court, I might ask why you didn't mention it at the first opportunity. Do you understand?" Summers asked.

Kelly nodded. Summers prompted for a verbal answer then asked her to state her name and tell her what had happened earlier that night. Kelly adhered to her request.

Before Summers could start on the interrogation process, Kelly asked if the boy was okay and pleaded her sympathies.

"I tried to stop him; I promise you. He was just a young boy."

Summers replied, "Kelly, the boy, Sean he is in a very bad way. A machine is currently breathing for him".

The news forced Kelly to burst into tears. Summers passed her a tissue whilst asking her what had happened.

Kelly sobbed as she told Summers her account of what had occurred in the restaurant, which matched that of the manager and diners. And her account of the altercation, which matched that of the eyewitnesses and the CCTV recording.

"So, Kelly, where did you go after the incident?" asked Summers. "We went around the corner and jumped in a taxi. The driver wasn't going to take us at first because it was a private hire, but Andrew gave him an extra twenty. When we got home, Andrew went out and told me to wash all of our clothes. But I couldn't, I just sat down, I couldn't even move. That poor boy," replied Kelly.

Summers noticed something that did not quite sit right. "Kelly, you have shown you are upset. I have sat across from hundreds of people and I know a liar, you are not one. However, something just does not add up, you did not mention Andrew until the taxi," said Summers in a puzzled manner.

The mention of her husband's name put the fear of God into Kelly. Shaking like a leaf, Kelly shot upright and looked over at the door while grabbing on to the side of her chair as if she were on a ride. Summers noticed her actions: sheer fear. This was not going to be a simple question and answer, this was a serious case of domestic abuse. Summers knew it would take a lot of willpower and determination on Kelly's behalf, if she was going to speak up about what happened that night. There was not enough time to ease the truth out of Kelly's mouth, it had to be prised out. Given there was only a forty-eight-hour window, Summers knew she had to be blunt, upfront and honest with Kelly.

"Right Mrs Blacks, I can clearly see you are upset and distressed. However, if you do not tell us your husband's part in this ordeal, I'm afraid you will be charged with assisting an offender, which could land you up to ten years in prison. The crime committed is horrific and I will not be held responsible for letting this man back on our streets."

Noticing Kelly's hesitation, Summers continued. "Now before you answer, I'm going to show you statements from the restaurant and then we will have a look at the CCTV footage. Then you can tell me if your husband really loves you."

Summers read extracts from different statements as she flicked through her file.

"She looked scared."

"It was almost like she had to ask for approval to breathe."

"She flinched every time he moved."

"She was very timid and hardly spoke."

"She would not make eye contact with any-one."

"He was aggressive."

"He spoke to her like she was rubbish."

"That poor woman."

Kelly was shocked, she did not even think there were that many people in the restaurant. She felt the heat flush in her face. Only partly because people pitied her, but more so because she thought she had been hiding it well.

Noticing Kelly's shame, Summers began to play the CCTV footage of Andrew assaulting her. Stopping the clip, Summers said to Kelly, "This man is beating you like an animal. In fact, no, I have seen animals treated better".

Kelly's head dropped to the floor while Summers spoke.

"Kelly, I can see with the way you curled up, how you are defending yourself. This was not the first time he has hit you, nor will it be the last time he hits you."

She nodded, a nod of submission. Summers knew, it was no longer a secret.

Summers continued the clip in slow motion as it approached the part where Andrew was pulling his leg back to kick her in the face.

"Kelly, you do understand if that kick had connected, you could have died. But instead, that young boy saved you. Yet...you still defend your husband, even though the boy is lying in intensive care fighting for his life. That could easily have been you," Summers said in disgust.

Click. The footage was paused on Sean's still body. Kelly stared, cupping her face in her hands as she cried. Silence loomed for a few minutes as Summers let it sink in before she continued.

"As it stands, you are just as much to blame as your husband is. You were there, you saw everything, yet you have not said that it was your husband. Imagine if this was your child lying there, alone, bleeding to death after selflessly trying to stop somebody from being hurt."

Kelly's emotions battled for the lead; shame, fear, anger, regret. What Summers said hit her hard, harder than her husband could dream of. To Summers and the officer, Kelly was not paying attention; she was just staring into space. But Kelly was seeing images of her daughter's face on the young boy's body. Her daughter was looking deep into her eyes, begging for her help. 'Please help me, please.'

Kelly was trying to escape the daydream, but her hands were covered in her own child's blood, leaving a stream down the cobbled path for the daydream to chase. As Kelly was about to reach a safe place, the path split and she fell into a pool of blood. The lights switched off and as Kelly sat there hugging her knees, she could hear her daughter begging for help.

Summers brought Kelly back to reality by placing her hand over hers, repeating her name, and assuring her safety. Then came the pivotal question of the interrogation.

"Kelly, what was Andrew like when you first met him?"

Kelly wiped the tears from her face and used the shock from her daydream to empower her to speak.

"When we met, we were young, we didn't have much other than love. We purchased our first flat together just after we were married. It was in the rough part of town, but it was our home. Not so long after we had our daughter. I think she was the reason for all Andrew's success. She gave him the inspiration, drive, and motivation. The fear of letting her down, made Andrew start his own plumbing business. It took sleepless nights and long hours but before we knew it, the company was turning over millions and millions of pounds. We went from having a little flat with hand-me-down furniture to having a big house, fancy cars, and luxury holidays. Life was great." Kelly's face lit up a little over the memory of how things had once been.

"It is true how the saying goes, 'with great success comes great responsibility' and I suppose people have different coping strategies to deal with it. It started with little things, like what I was wearing. I would get ready and Andrew would make remarks like, 'Are you going downtown or shopping?' The insults grew more negative and fouler as time went by, until they came every day.

I got to such a low point I would wear black trousers that were too big, to hide the shape of my body and a blouse. It was the same blouse but three different colours. Sad, I know, but a little change of colour cheered me up. I even went as far as to stop wearing makeup, only putting it on at Andrew's request." The light from the happy memories soon drifted away.

"It was a very hard time for me, I felt so worthless, I forgot how to feel pretty. The only thing that kept me going was my freedom, as Andrew was working a lot. I was able to get my hair and nails done, see my friends. But that was not for long. The remarks weren't only about my appearance now, they were also aimed at me meeting men. This was so far from the truth. I couldn't sit there anymore and get accused of such dreadful things.

Finally, I stood up for myself, which would prove to be the first and last, for some time.

Andrew had come home early from work; I had been to get my hair done. The girls at the salon saw I was down so they did me a little modelling session. They cut my hair shorter, and a different colour, it was like a rose gold. I had my makeup done, it was beautiful, the makeup artist did a great job. The contour matched my skin, the shadowing on my eye-lids went from dark to light purple. My lips were the darkest of purple, they almost looked black. I even had a few glasses of prosecco. I enjoyed that day so much, I remembered what it felt like to feel pretty again."

Pressed for time, Summers looked at the clock. Kelly caught her eye and turned to see what Summers was looking at. She let out a cry of pain as she moved her bruised sides. She realised Summers had checked the clock and continued, speaking faster now.

"Pulling up on the drive, I was a little shocked to see Andrew was back early. I was scared to go in, as I didn't know how he would act. I intended on wiping the makeup off before I saw him. I opened the door and went into the kitchen and threw my keys down on the stone island.

As I was about to turn to go into the front room, Andrew was stood there blocking my path. He was asking me all kinds of stupid questions, implying I was having an affair. I told him he was paranoid, and it was all in his head. I remember looking into his eyes, the look in Andrew's eyes was different, he looked evil. He hit me in the face like I was a punch bag, the force knocking me unconscious momentarily. I sat there on the floor holding my cheek. As I tried to get up, he hit me again and again. Each time, my head bouncing off the floor. The pain became too much, everything went black.

I could see the tiles on my kitchen floor, but my vision was flickering like when an old strobe light comes on. I had passed out. I tried to jump up as soon as possible, but I found it hard to move. My face was pounding, and my sides were so tender. Tender to touch even. After a struggle, I managed to find my feet and climbed the stairs before collapsing on my bed.

The next morning, I woke up in my nightwear with a damp towel on my face. I tried to get up but couldn't, the pain was too much. I let out a loud 'ouch!'. Andrew heard and came rushing in. He was so apologetic and sweet. He promised me it would never happen again. For the next three days, I stayed in bed and he waited on me hand and foot. He even bought me flowers. I forgave him. When our daughter came in, I said I had fallen down the stairs.

Looking back, I should not have let my daughter see me like that. But Andrew made a mistake. A one-off. It would never happen again.

Unfortunately, Andrew's possessive ways grew worse. I am not allowed a phone; I must stay in when he is out. If I went to the shop, Andrew would wait outside in the car. You never guess what though, I get to wear makeup more often. Not to feel pretty though, to cover up the bruising from when Andrew hit me. He lied when he said he would never do it again.

I see it on the TV, you are told to leave an abusive relationship. But leave to where? Who would look after my daughter? How would we live? I've managed to hide all of this from her, it would really break her heart if she found out."

By this time, Kelly was a complete mess. Not even a dam could hold back her tears. Then she said the words Summer was waiting on. At first she was blubbering, making it extremely difficult to understand what she was saying. Summers asked if she could repeat it. Kelly did, loud and clear.

"He did it, he stabbed that young boy for no reason."

Summers and the other officer could see that she was living her life in fear of Andrew. And it was visible to see what would have happened to her if she did not leave with her husband. Domestic abuse really hit a nerve with Summers.

After bringing the custody officer up to date, they decided to release Kelly on bail for eight weeks, for assisting an offender. Her only bail condition was not to go near the restaurant.

Andrew meanwhile used his time alone self-ishly, by banging on the door and shouting abuse at everyone that passed. The sergeant informed him he was about to be taken in for questioning and asked if he wanted a solicitor.

"A solicitor for what, self-defence. Get a grip," Andrew protested.

The four officers pulled Andrew from his holding cell and put him in a seat in the interrogation room, handcuffing him to the table to limit his movement. DCI Summers followed the same introduction process as she had with Kelly and asked Andrew for his sequence of events, starting with the incident at the restaurant.

Andrew made out like nothing was his fault, in total denial. The incident in the restaurant happened because the waiter was rude to his wife more than once. And he swore that he could not just sit there while somebody was disrespectful to her.

"Andrew, if that was the case then why did you stomp off and leave your wife? If the waiter was doing what you said, wouldn't you have left with your wife to ensure her safety, as a gentleman would?" asked Summers.

Andrew's excuse was that his head went due to being so angry and if he would have waited around for his wife, he may have hit one of the men. Summers knew it was a lie as it did not match the other statements. But she wanted to catch him out, asking inquisitively, "So, if that was the case then Mr Blacks, why did you assault your wife further up the road?"

Andrew replied, "She makes me sick, hanging around with all the men when I walked off, she has no loyalty".

Summers pointed out that Andrew went from being a true gentleman, to a villain in less than ten seconds. Moreover, a villain who thought there was a good enough excuse for beating up his wife. A pure and utterly disgusted tone raised from Summers' voice box while Andrew stayed silent.

In the hope Andrew would show some remorse for his actions, Summers asked, "So the young boy, why stab him?"

Andrew did not bat an eyelid with his response. "Do you really think someone can knock me to the ground? Some little boy who thought he was a gangster because he had a knife. Not a chance, if I did not put it in him, he would have put it in me."

Raising her eyebrow, Summers interrupted. "Andrew, you act like this was some hoodlum that set up on you in the street for no reason. He was protecting your wife, as you should have."

Andrew was furious, he pulled his hands to try and break free from the handcuffs. The officer next to Summers flinched. Andrew looked dead in Summers' eye and said, "And look where being a knight in shining armour got him."

"So, Andrew, we can conclude that all of this was because your ego was bruised, as with your eye, by the looks of it," said the officer.

Andrew started to smirk; he was about to laugh because he believed, when all is said and done, he would come out victorious.

BANG, DCI Summers hit the table with both hands while standing up. She leant over in Andrew's face and said quietly, "You are nothing but a bully, a little man, I do not fear you".

Still smirking, Andrew sat back. A knock at the door interrupted, the door was opened slightly.

"DCI Summers, can I have a word please."

Summers looked Andrew dead in the eye as she paused the tape, she then left the room.

Summer muttered, "This man is seriously rubbing me up the wrong way".

"Ma'am, he has died."

So enraged by Andrew's behaviour, she asked her colleague who he meant.

"The young boy Ma'am, Sean."

Summers' head dropped. Shaking her head, she said, "That poor boy."

"It's such a shame."

In a rage, Summers said, "That man in there is nothing short of an animal."

Her colleague said, "Ma'am," in a sharp and authoritative manner.

Summers looked up. Her colleague looked at the door.

"He's still in there. Now, go and get that boy the justice he deserves."

Summer took a deep breath, removing Andrew from beneath her skin. "I will, don't you worry. Thank you for the update."

Swearing underneath her breath, Summers returned to the room. Silence as she sat down, she cleared her throat before continuing.

"Well Mr Blacks, I'm afraid to say the attempted murder charge has been increased to a murder charge. The young boy you stabbed has just died."

The smirk on Andrew's face dropped. His mouth was wide open like a tunnel. All the tension that had built in the room vanished like it was never there.

Andrew was advised he would be remanded in prison until his court date. He attempted to speak, but Summers and the officer got up and left the interrogation room.

Just before the door closed, she whispered, "I'm sure your daughter will love to hear how her dad is a woman-beating MURDERER!"

The door closed, but the sound of Andrew banging and yelling of abuse could be heard throughout the entire police station.

NINE

YOUNG LOVE

Kelly was released on bail; Summers requested that a police officer escorted her back home, which was under armed guard as they did not know if there would be any retaliation attacks. Kelly's main priority was to make sure her daughter did not find out about what had happened until after she had been back to answer bail. By that time, Kelly would know more about what was happening, with her bail arrangements.

More importantly, if Andrew was coming back, it would allow her to make necessary arrangements if the worst of things could happen. This expectation would soon become short-lived.

After hatching a plan to temporarily cover up the night's events, Kelly sat down with a cup of tea to watch TV.

She was greeted by the news: 'breaking story' in white, with a post-box red background, the text took over the whole TV screen. The title faded out, the presenter appeared sitting at a white desk, and people blurred in the background.

With a saddening look on his face and sorrow in his voice, he announced, "Yet another young life taken by knife crime. A teenager was stabbed in the town centre yesterday evening. He was taken to the hospital; but despite their efforts, they could not save him. He was known locally as Sean. Police have made two arrests".

While he spoke, a picture of Sean appeared, panning in from the left. Kelly froze, dropping her cup of tea in shock. The cup dropped faster than the tea, making the tea look like it was hanging mid-air, like the lava in a lava lamp. The cup hit the granite floor and broke into pieces resembling Kelly's heart. The only part intact was the handle, spinning while the tea splashed all over the kitchen cupboards.

She could not believe what she had just seen, the young boy was dead, her husband a murderer. Looking at the picture of Sean, Kelly began to have flashbacks from the night. She was trembling, she was scared, she was broken.

Hannah had waited and waited for Sean at the party but as he did not show, nor did he answer his phone. She decided enough was enough, she left the party and went back to her friends to stay the night. Having been entertained by her friends with embarrassing stories, funny videos, and girl chat, she put Sean to the back of her mind, until it was time for lights out.

She found it hard to settle down and sleep as she knew how much the night meant to her and the important conversation approaching. Tears of loneliness dampened the pillow under her face. She fell asleep with the thoughts of Sean in the arms of some other girl at the party. Regret took over, maybe she should have made their relationship public sooner. Then, that way Sean would have been with her all of the time and there would be no need to be so secretive about their love.

It was the early hours of the morning, Hannah's body was being shaken violently from left to right, she felt like she was on a boat. She could hear her name being called, it was a worried voice, a voice in distress.

"What's up?" she asked as she rubbed her eyes.

"It's Sean," the voice said.

"What is he here?" Hannah asked. She leaned up and pulled a band off her wrist to pull her hair back for the chance of looking as presentable as possible with such little sleep.

"No," her friend responded, "HE IS DEAD".

Hannah waited a minute in the hope she would wake from this nightmare, the moment never came.

"How? Who told you? Is it even true?" Hannah asked her friend.

"It was on the news, here," she replied, passing her phone over.

Hannah retrieved the phone, trembling like a washing machine on high speed, she had to use two hands to keep it stable. Tears rolled out of Hannah's eyes. Her tears colliding with the phone but she did not care. Her friend put her arm around her shoulder and brought her head to her chest.

"Hannah, there is another video, but I don't think you should see it."

Judging by the current events, Hannah felt that it could not get any worse. She clicked on the link to the video. Right before her eyes was

Sean lying there. Eyes closed. Still. Hannah could not watch any more, she had an intense sickening feeling in her stomach. She hurled the phone and broke free of her friend's grip.

Running into the bathroom she slid across the floor on her knees, before stopping at the toilet basin. Putting her head in the toilet, she began to throw up. After discarding last night's chicken and chips, Hannah thought that she would feel better. But the feeling of sickness hovered in the pit of her stomach, refusing to leave. Her stomach tensed, wrenching, trying to rid her body of the feeling. Blotches of popped blood vessels appeared on Hannah's face from the pressure of retching. Her friend propped up against the bathroom door, watching, not knowing what to do: she phoned Hannah a taxi home.

Pulling together enough strength to get to her feet, but still weak, Hannah used her hands to guide her to the sink. Struggling to turn the tap on, she became frustrated. Her cries could now be heard even downstairs and others began appearing at the door. Leaning on the sink with her forearms she was too weak to pull up her head. But was it because of the lack of strength or was it the guilt that prevented her from looking at herself in the mirror?

A black cab pulled up outside her friend's house and beeped the horn twice. Unable to see straight and in a dizzy state, her shoulder scraped the walls keeping her upright. Hannah collected her bag and went to the taxi. Not registering the farewell from her friend and her family, Hannah slumped in the rear of the car. Hannah knew what she wanted. What she needed. She required love and nurturing, the type of love and nurturing only somebody close to her could provide. She needed her mother.

As the black cab approached her house, Hannah's mind was in no fit state to notice the dark blue surveillance truck on the end of her road, the armed guards parked outside in a big black four-wheel-drive vehicle, or the police that checked the taxi driver's identification before they let him pull onto the drive. The driver of the taxi eased on the breaks, bringing the black cab to a complete stand still outside her house.

Hannah, still traumatized, ever so slowly, departed out of the taxi, hugging her bag close to her chest. Her hair looked as if it had not seen a brush in days, her eyelids puffy from so much crying. Last night's mascara had run down her cheeks like a river, making her face look like something from a horror movie. She walked in a zombie-like state to the house, scraping her fluffy Ugg slippers across the ground. Staring forward but looking at nothing. Only by her mind switching into autopilot was she able to unlock the door and get inside without stumbling into anything.

Kelly could hear something sliding on the hard surface of the hallway floor. She turned down the TV and tilted her head to increase her hearing. Shh. Shh. The noise grew louder. SHH. SHH. Kelly unlocked her crossed legs and went to inspect the noise, crouching low to the ground like a ninja. Slowly poking her head out of the door, Kelly saw her daughter but something was wrong with her. Kelly's hands climbed up the wall until she was vertical, observing her daughter dragging her feet like she had no energy to pick them up. SHH. SHH.

"Hannah, are you okay?" Kelly asked in a worried tone.

No response. Kelly approached Hannah with caution until she was directly in front of her. Bending down, Kelly looked right into Hannah's face, again asking if she was okay but receiving only silence again. By now, Hannah had stopped moving forward but her mind was still racing.

As Hannah looked right through her mother, Kelly saw something was amiss. She guided her into the comfort of the living room, assuring her everything was going to be okay. As a mother, Kelly knew that it was time to push her own issues to the side like a heavy rock and be strong for herself and her daughter.

Guiding Hannah to the settee, Kelly continued to ask her if she was okay. Slowly moving the bag from Hannah's grasp, Hannah's eyes turned towards her mother making eye contact.

"MMMum, he's de..." Hannah stuttered before placing her head between her mother's neck and collarbone. She could not bring herself to say it.

Kelly cradled her daughter and asked her to repeat herself. Asking, "What is the matter Hannah, what has got you in this mess?"

A few moments of silence were finally broken by Hannah telling her mother that Sean was dead. Kelly's heart stopped, she found it hard to breathe. Questions were entering her brain at a rapid pace. However, two questions appeared at the forefront: how did Hannah know Sean? But more importantly, how was she going to tell Hannah it was her father who had killed him. Kelly's plans were well and truly out of the window. But one thing remained, she needed to find out what the connection between Hannah and Sean was.

Hannah sobbed and sobbed while in her mother's arms. Kelly cupped her ear as she did when she was younger, knowing it would comfort her. Hannah was trying to tell her mother everything, but Kelly could barely make out a word. Words joined with sobs and sobs with cries of explanations. One thing was for certain, Kelly had never seen her daughter act like this over any boy before.

The flood of emotions had made Hannah tired; she fell asleep in her mum's arms. This was the perfect opportunity for Kelly to find out the connection between the two. She laid Hannah down on the settee and covered her with the softest of blankets. She watched as Hannah laid there snuggled into the blanket. She was restless and looked pale, like she had aged ten years since Kelly last saw her.

Kelly crept out of the kitchen on her tiptoes, being careful not to make any floorboards creak. She started her search in Hannah's college bag, trying to find a connection, tags indicating their relationship in a book, or anything hinting at who Sean was to her daughter.

Kelly soon realised where she was going wrong. She was thinking about it as if it was her when she was at school, but times had since moved on.

She needed access to Hannah's phone, which was impossible. So, she hunted through her social media accounts. She had Sean on most of her accounts but there was no interaction between the two. This made little sense to Kelly. Recognising her failure, she would have to wait until Hannah had woken up to find out what was happening.

Hannah became unsettled, signalling she was about to wake. Kelly prepared a cup of tea for when she woke. After putting sugar in the cup, she banged the spoon on the edge of the cup. Ting, ting, ting. Not realizing how loud the sound was, Hannah woke up. Kelly smiled softly and continued to make the brews. Picking up the hot cup by the handle, she placed her free hand underneath the cup to prevent any spillage. Hannah shuffled upright to retrieve the drink, using two hands to hug the cup: bringing warmth to her stone-cold body.

The sleep had calmed Hannah, she was still upset but no longer in a state of shock. Kelly sat down next to her, cupping her hands.

"Was the young boy that died your friend?"

Hannah nodded and began to smile. Kelly knew from her smile that this was not just any old friend. Kelly carried on, asking how long Hannah had known him for.

Hannah replied, "I've known him for some years, but we have been seeing each other for nearly a year. Mum you would have loved him, he was so funny and smart".

Hannah's face glowed when she spoke of him. "Dad would love him too, where is he?"

Kelly promptly brushed the question off by saying he was away for work and asked

Hannah to share more about Sean. It was killing Kelly inside witnessing how much the two had obviously been in love, knowing her husband had taken that from her. On top of that, also keeping the secret from Hannah, ripped Kelly from the inside out.

Thinking of her future, Hannah told her mum she could not live without Sean.

"You will be okay Hannah, you're still very young. You still have the rest of your life to live," said Kelly, trying to bring some positivity to the horrifying situation.

Hannah sat thinking, "It isn't that easy, Mum. Dad is still here."

"Of course it's not Hannah, you have been through a lot. But in twenty years' time you will look at it as a distant memory."

However, Hannah's reply would change the lives of all those affected by that knife, that night. Hannah threw both arms around her mum and cried, "Mum, I'm pregnant".

TEN

REST IN PEACE

The hours that passed while Charlotte was in the hospital were the hardest that she had ever succumbed to. Deep down in the darkest part of her gut, Charlotte knew her son had gone. But she had hope and until her hope was gone, she would remain at his side. Unfortunately, the hope deteriorated rapidly.

The machines keeping Sean alive periodically moved, so much so the gust of air being pumped into Sean's lungs became a background noise to Charlotte's ears. This was until the machine started to move faster and faster. Becoming more aware of her surroundings, she noticed the beep of the heart rate monitor had started to slow down. She panicked, opening the door she yelled for help.

A doctor came to her aid with his coat flowing like a cape. He looked at Sean and frowned. He took his observations and viewed his notes before asking Charlotte to take a seat.

"Ms Barkly, I am afraid to inform you that Sean's condition is deteriorating. Our observations and test results have shown that he is brain dead. This was due to the lack of oxygen to his brain. The machines are keeping him alive. And although Sean looks peacefully asleep, there are no signs of life: he is not dead but may never wake up."

Charlotte could not face adding to the pain that Sean had already succumbed to. The doctor left, giving Charlotte some time to think. After an hour of pacing up and down, talking to herself and to Sean, she made the brave decision to turn off the life support.

The doctor returned, approving of Charlotte's choice as that was the best thing to do. He then went behind the machine and apologised before discretely turning off the life support machine and waited, ready to record the time of death. As the noise of the life support machine stopped, Charlotte held Sean's hand whilst sat on the edge of his bed.

Charlotte's final words to her beloved son went, "Son, I tried to bring you up in a safe place. I cannot fault you for carrying a knife with the amount of knife crime in today's society. But look where it got you. It's not your fault though, it is mine. I shouldn't have let you down, it was my duty as a parent, to keep you safe and I failed. I'm sure the heavens will welcome another angel. Goodbye Son, love you always."

The beeps of the heart rate machine grew further apart, the next beep adding a little bit of hope. She gave him a kiss on his head, that was the last beep.

Charlotte was informed that Sean's body would not be released from the mortuary for another six weeks, as an autopsy would need to be completed. This gave her the time to plan a proper funeral, a send-off fit for her beloved son. All to be focused on what he liked.

To take herself and Sean's closest friends to and from the church, Charlotte chose a big black stretched four-wheel drive, with chrome bull bars and handles. The interior was black leather with silver stitching and lights that twinkled like stars in the roof. When Sean was younger, he used to love the yellow version, so Charlotte thought it would be what he wanted.

His coffin was beech oak, not far from the colour of cardboard. Knowing Sean would call this 'weak', she hired a local graffiti artist to spray the coffin to replicate a rocket as Sean always wanted to become an aerospace engineer. The finished piece looked excellent. It was all metallic silver, with a red dome at the top and fire coming from the bottom, it was so realistic and intricate. It even had a little window, in this was a picture of Sean winking with his thumb up. The thought of Sean's approval brought a tear to his mother's eye.

The church she chose was beautiful. The drive leading up to it was peaceful with short grass covering either side and trees following the road right up to the entrance of the church. Each stained-glass window told a different story that came alive when the sun's rays touched it.

Inside, it was just one large room, with an altar at the front and seats covering the floor. Only dark wooden beams and dark cast-iron chandeliers decorated the ceiling. Charlotte's only doubt was that the room was too big, and its emptiness might look as if her son did not have many friends.

For the wake, she had hired out the function room in the local community centre. Charlotte knew Sean loved his music, but she had no idea where to start. She got in touch with Kiki and asked her to help arrange a DJ and MCs. She wanted the night to end in a show dedicated to Sean. Rest assured, Kiki fulfilled the request on one condition, that she could say a few words at Sean's funeral. Charlotte agreed. The final step was his headstone that could not be laid until he had been buried, but she knew what he would have wanted.

The headstone was black granite with sparkling fragments, that shone like stars, when touched with light. It stood at four feet tall and had a step up to it. Its top came out around two feet and was the shape of an arch. To support the top of the headstone were two columns shaped like rockets, one on each side. The front of the structure had Sean's name, his date of birth under a picture of a sunrise and death underneath the picture of a sunset. Below the silver text was a picture of Sean grinning like a Cheshire cat, showing all of his teeth. His smile was so big, it stretched across the width of the structure. Underneath that, a small passage was written by Charlotte.

'The light of my life, you will be missed dearly. You will live on through those you touched. The most polite and helpful person. The heavens have gained another angel. Love you always.'

Days turned into nights; weekdays forged into weekends as Charlotte waited to be able to lay her son to rest. The day finally arrived. She wore a black blouse that had a leopard print covering the front and gold buttons. She chose that top as Sean bought it for her and referred to it as her 'pulling top'. They would laugh every time she wore it. Accompanying her blouse, was a black skirt and leopard print shoes to match her top.

Kiki and a few others were in the front room waiting with her for the hearse to arrive. They were all in hysterics, sharing silly stories of Sean. The one that wedged in Charlotte's mind was when he pranked one of his friends. Sean thought it would be funny to dress up like a zombie and get in a lift with his friend, knowing that he did not like zombie films. Anyway, the fear caused his friend to urinate himself in the lift. Charlotte smiled as she wondered how she could give birth to such a funny guy, that shared energy everywhere he went.

"Ms Barkly, the hearse is outside," Kiki said, while picking up her jacket.

Charlotte took a deep breath and headed to the front door. As the door opened, the black hearse came into view causing her to freeze. She never thought this day would happen. She felt like she could manipulate it, obviously she could not. But if she could, she would rewind it to the day Sean took the knife out the drawer.

The thought of him having to carry a knife sent shivers down her entire body, causing her to jolt, like you do when you are asleep and fall off something. She soon came back to reality and proceeded out of the house to take a closer look at the hearse.

Floral letter tributes surrounded the coffin: Son, Sean, and Miss You. All outlined with birds of paradise. It gave the effect that the edges were moving, so vibrantly. Coupling them were dark black roses, a complete con-trast to the warm and bright day. And finally, in the centre, like a beam of sun, were bright orange roses. Charlotte could hear Kiki and the rest of Sean's friends say how good they looked, commenting that Sean would call them 'fire'.

They all bundled into the stretched four-wheel-drive and put on their seat belts. They requested the driver pass them the aux cable so they could play Sean's playlist. Singing and dancing along to the songs, they were having so much fun. Charlotte could not understand half of what was being said but rolled her eyes at any rude remarks she could make out. Not taking away the pain her heart was in, she was so grounded by the impact Sean's life had on other people.

She knew her son would not be forgotten. Turning her head to look out of the window, Charlotte could see bystanders stop and look at the hearse. Understanding, that to them it was just another body, but to her it was the one thing she thought she would have until the day she died.

Pulling up to the church, the vehicle came to a standstill. Then a huge cheer erupted, Charlotte lowered the window to see what was happening. Before her, stood a sea of people come to support her son. She could not believe it, hundreds and hundreds of people. This was confirmation that she had raised a good person.

The vehicles slowly crept up the drive until they arrived at the entrance to the church. Kiki and the rest of the friends exited the four-wheel-drive first to go to the hearse for the coffin. On their signal, Charlotte got out and then led the coffin into the church. Entering the church, to the sound of Sean's favourite song, the crowd stood as they clapped to the beat of the song. This is what Sean would have wanted, a celebration of his life. Not the mourning of his death.

Charlotte spotted a few tears on familiar faces, but everyone was smiling. She was weak and exhausted, but the energy created by Sean gave her the power to walk down the aisle. An aisle that Sean should have walked down on his wedding day. As the casket was at the front of the altar, Charlotte, Kiki, and friends took a seat at the front. Once seated, the guests that had seats sat down.

The music faded out while the Vicar prepared his notes. Silence...The Vicar's voice was very strong, it could reach people far and wide.

"Let us begin with the Lord's Prayer."

All participants dropped their heads, some prayed along with the Vicar.

"Our Father,
who art in heaven,
hallowed be thy name,
thy kingdom come,
thy will be done,
on Earth as it is in heaven.
Give us this day our daily bread,
and forgive us our trespasses,
as we forgive those who trespass against us.
And lead us not into temptation,
but deliver us from evil.
For the kingdom, the power,
and the glory,
now and forever.
Amen."

The crowd replied Amen in harmony as they all lifted their heads. The Vicar cleared his throat with a grunt.

"I bring you here today to celebrate the life of Sean Barkly. Loving son, brother, grandson, and friend. Sean was a very intelligent and polite young man, who took it upon himself to put others first. I am sure God will be graced with his presence. Before we hear words from Sean's friend, mother, and teacher, I would like to take this opportunity to talk about the current issue we are having.

Unfortunately, I am laying to rest many young people as a result of knife crime. Here we have a young boy who was not violent, or in a gang. But he felt he had to carry a knife for protection as he was in fear of his life, due to the barbaric behaviour that has somehow become acceptable amongst our society. A decision that led to him losing his life.

Grandparents, parents, and carers, we must talk to our young people of today and let them know of the consequences of carrying a knife. A decision can be made in a split-second but get it wrong and your life could change forever. To enable you to envision the true scalability of what I mean, take a moment and put yourself in Sean's position. Imagine being at your own funeral. Imagine how the people who love you the most would feel. Imagine the hurt, the pain, the agony of them no longer being able to see you."

The powerful words of the Vicar touched people old and young, many were visibly fighting back the tears. As the Vicar continued, they were conquered by their emotions. Tears dropped; tissues caught them. Charlotte looked around and saw the upset that had spread throughout the church. At first, she was agitated, but after the words of the Vicar sunk in, she understood why he had done it. It was a plea to stop knife crime, from the view of loved ones, not the young people themselves.

The Vicar welcomed Kiki to the altar. Instead of a speech, Kiki had written a heartfelt poem as she knew the flow of her words would guide her through the rough waters ahead. Stepping up, she attracted a lot of attention as she was wearing a dress and makeup, something nobody had seen as she was always in a tracksuit. Moving the microphone closer to her mouth, she began:

"To Sean, my brother from another mother.

**My friend, my friend, my friend,
until we meet again.**
From the first day you came to the ends,
I knew we would be friends.

113

Never in my darkest days, would I think to
say,
that you had been taken away.

**My friend, my friend, my friend,
until we meet again.**
We could argue in the AM, not talk in the PM,
but we always remained friends.
Now you are gone, it all feels so wrong,
My life is like a broken song.

**My friend, my friend, my friend,
until we meet again.**
Even though you're not here, can I make it
clear,
You know that we're still friends.
Sitting above the weather, we're still to-
gether,
Forget about you, I could never.

**My friend, my friend, my friend,
until we meet again.**
Laughing and dissing, part of me is missing,
A part just for you, my friend.
Kicking a bit of footy, chilling after study,
Cold nights with hats and a hoody.

**My friend, my friend, my friend,
until we meet again.**
If I could rewind seconds, I'd tell you to leave
that weapon,

That would be my advice, my friend.
We had big dreams of big cars and nice
jeans,
We were the A team.

**My friend, my friend, my friend,
until we meet again.**
I know things won't be the same, but when
people mention your name,
I'll tell them you're my best of friends.
With you I believed, now it's almost impossi-
ble to achieve,
Without you next to me.

**My friend, my friend, my friend,
until we meet again.**
No more buses to college, to gain the
knowledge,
Oh boy, these feeling hurts.
I know your true worth, now you're no longer
on Earth,
Oh boy, I feel cursed.

**My friend, my friend, my friend,
until we meet again.**

The mourners were moved. Kiki's tears
dropped on the paper smudging the ink. But
she did not just read those words, she felt
them: they were etched into her heart.

Sean's teacher Mr Woodhead took to the altar,
thanking Kiki for her beautiful poem.

115

Confirming that he had seen the strong friendship form between the two.

"I taught Sean right the way through high school. He was good in class, well for the most part. He did like to create, let's say, a fun environment in the classroom. Including acts such as arriving to class wearing a bright pink wig he had found and requesting he go by the name of his female alter ego: Sasha."

The story brought on a barrage of laughter from Sean's friends and old classmates.

"As for his personality, I could only add to the fantastic things already said about Sean. I am here for a purpose, to tell you all our beloved Sean was accepted on to NASA's aerospace engineering programme. Sean was the first person ever from England to reach the program which is an exceptional achievement. It involved him going over to America for four years and returning as a qualified aerospace engineer, including a university degree."

The news brought forward a clap of congratulations from the crowd.

"Why am I telling you? What can we take away from this achievement? Although super smart, Sean knew he had to work hard to achieve success. That is something every single person here today can do. Now, do not let Sean's life, Sean's legacy, go to waste. His life must continue now with each one of you. We must reach our goals, not only for ourselves but for Sean as he was and still is on our team, wanting us to succeed.

Charlotte stood up and walked to the altar for the final words of the service. "I would like to thank you all for coming and being with me while we say our final goodbye to Sean. My baby boy, you are in a safe place now. This cruel world can hurt you no longer. Your life will be celebrated and never mourned. Keep watching over me."

She could speak no more, feeling weak and becoming unsteady. The Vicar came to Charlotte's help before she collapsed and held her up. He asked if she wanted to continue but she could not. Kiki, came up to the altar and retrieved Charlotte, taking her back to her seat.

The Vicar was bringing the service to an end with a prayer. Just as everyone dropped their heads to begin, the door of the church opened. Catching everyone's attention, the whole church turned their heads. A silhouette shackled at the feet and hands entered. As the figure approached, there was a police officer bound to each arm. Gasps waved through the crowd and whispers began. The figure walked down the aisle and stopped in front of the casket.

To Charlotte, the figure went by the name of Michael. To young Sean, it had been 'big brother' and to the crowd 'Big Juj'. For those that did not know, a sense of confusion sparked but for those who did, a sense of evil immersed them, even in a place of God.

Big Juj raised his eyes to the Vicar and instructed him to continue. As their eyes met, the victor felt uneasy, forcing him to bow his head and start to pray. Everyone's head dropped apart from Big Juj, like he did not answer to the same god as anyone else in that room. Total disrespect.

"Let us bow our heads to the Lord,
for he will guide Sean to the heavens above.
May Sean's manners and warm heart,
protect him on his journey to the Lord.
May his helpful soul and positive energy,
work as fuel to get him there faster.
And allow our prayers to bring peace to Sean
as he rests:
Rest in peace young man.
Amen."

The service came to an end, Big Juj attempted to go and carry the coffin but the officers pulled on the chains causing them to rattle as they shook their heads.

He cursed under his breath and said, "RIP little bro".

Then he was escorted out of the church to the burial followed by Charlotte, the casket, and the guests as Sean's song was played again.

Charlotte did not have the energy to worry about what people thought about her because of the actions of her eldest son. She was just happy to see him, she had no one, and she needed some support.

Deep down she knew that if Michael were in Sean's life, he would not have become a victim of such a cowardly crime. Nobody in their right mind would of hurt him, especially with Michael's reputation. Charlotte began to feel guilty; Michael had done a lot of bad things to others but never to family. With him, his family was safe.

ELEVEN

TOO LATE TO TURN BACK

It took over an hour for everyone to gather around the place of burial. The graveyard was jam-packed with people and cars: it had never been so busy. Directly around the grave stood the Vicar, Charlotte, Michael with his escorts, Kiki and the rest of Sean's close friends. In a space between Kiki and Michael, was a mound of earth that was taken from the grave.

Even though there was a great mass of people, the only noises were lawnmowers and the blackbirds with yellow beaks singing to each other in the trees.

Sean stood behind the Vicar, a few rows back, meaning his vision of the casket was blocked. He had no idea what was going on. He looked around and caught a glimpse of his mother, he shouted to her, but she did not answer. He did the same with Kiki and all the rest of his friends but still, he received no answer. He asked himself what was going on. Every single person looked so serious, what had he missed? He walked over to his mum and also noticed the man in the handcuffs. Everything was so strange.

Standing a few rows behind his mum, Sean heard a man he did not recognise say, "Mum, everything will be okay", whilst grabbing her hand in comfort.

Wait, am I in a dream? Is this the future? Sean asked himself.

This theory was found to be false as his mum looked the same as she did yesterday, and she was wearing her pulling top. He was adamant she would not have cherished that top so much that she kept it until he was that old.

Sean swam through the crowd over to his mother. He extended his hand to catch his mother's attention. Just as he expected her to turn around, Sean's hand went straight through her shoulder. He pulled back and shook it like it like it was on fire to confirm it was attached to the rest of his body.

He tried to touch the person behind him, the same thing happened. He started to feel anxious, was he in a dream? Was this a nightmare? Were these people even his family? Was this all a joke? Sean began to run at people and scream in their face, but no one reacted. No one could see or hear him. While he was screaming at people, trying to get their attention, he missed the Vicar speaking.

"In sure and certain hope of the resurrection to eternal life, through Our Lord Jesus Christ, we commend to Almighty God, Sean and we commit his body to the ground."

Sean finally noticed that everyone was facing the same direction. He moved around them to see what everybody was staring at. As he got closer, he heard the Vicar say, 'earth to earth,' while throwing some earth into a large hole. When the earth hit whatever was inside, it brought Sean to his knees. It sounded so loud, like a bomb had been activated. Sean grabbed his ears to stop the ringing from the loud noise as he struggled on the ground.

The Vicar continued with 'ashes to ashes' and threw more earth down the hole. This time, Sean struggled to get off his knees. He begged for the Vicar to stop but the man could not hear him and continued until, 'Amen'. This last time the Vicar threw earth into the hole, Sean could not get up at all, he felt as if he were being forced to the ground like the world was on his shoulders.

Sean needed to see what was down that hole. With no other option but to crawl, he moved forward on his hands and knees. His hand grabbed on to the edge of the hole as he fought against the force. Using all his might, he managed to pull himself up enough to peak over the edge to see what all the fuss was about.

Staring back at him, was the picture of himself on the casket. Instantly, Sean flashed back to the night he passed away. White Air Force Ones. The knife in his waistband. Punching a man. A sharp, painful feeling in his neck. Looking up at a familiar woman. The sound of the helicopter. The shock on his chest. His mum's soft voice. Feeling peaceful.

Sean tried to pat himself to see if he was real, his hands did not make a connection with his body. He screamed, he begged, and he prayed that he did not die that terrible night. But it was too late, the damage was done. There was nothing he could do or say, he was dead. Nothing could bring him back.

As each person came and threw a handful of earth on his grave, he walked over to speak to his mum to give her his final goodbye. And although he knew she could not hear him, he had to do it.

"Mum, I'm so sorry for what I have done. I feel so embarrassed for what I have put you through. I didn't mean to get stabbed; I promise. I took that knife to protect myself, I never intended to use it. It was for my safety. I wasn't into anything bad, you did not raise a bad lad, honest. I know you taught me to mind my own business, but I couldn't just leave that woman there to get beat like that, I just couldn't.

I can't thank you enough for all you have done for me. You supported me so much, even when you needed supporting yourself. You are my rock, my role model. I promised myself I would never make you suffer, and I would do well for the both of us. I planned on getting you off the estate and living in the countryside somewhere. Where we would be woken up by the sound of cockerels. But that cannot happen now, I have failed you, I have failed me, I have failed the both of us. I hope one day you will forgive me; I am sorry."

He kissed his mother on the cheek and went in search of Kiki.

"Yes Kiki, check you out in that dress. Who are you trying to impress?" Sean said as he chuckled to himself. "Man, I'm sorry that all this has happened. That you're having to do all of this. I can see that you and the man dem invited a lot of people. Thank you. I didn't think I had so many friends. I was on the way to meet you at the party and a madness happened.

I saw what happened to that guy on the news and when I heard Daniel got stabbed, I got real paranoid. Cha, enough of that, look right, you just focus on your dreams, for the both of us. Don't get distracted by any guys. And don't carry no weapons or get involved in any badness. My friend, until we meet again."

Sean could feel his time was up, he yelled, 'I'm sorry' one last time and gave his soul rest. As he was rising, he noticed everyone had left except for his mum. She was approached by a young woman. It was Hannah.

"Hello Mrs Barkly," she said.

Charlotte looked at Hannah and smiled, expecting that she was just showing her respects, and would leave but she did not.

"I don't know how to tell you this, but I'm Sean's partner."

Charlotte did not want to be rude but also did not know what to say as Sean had never mentioned her before.

Hannah continued, "We have been seeing each other for almost a year. The night when Sean was killed, I had arranged to meet him to tell him something".

Charlotte's interest promptly spiked as to what she was about to hear. Getting worked up, finding it hard to speak, Hannah spouted the news out along with a cry.

"I was planning to tell him that I'm pregnant."

Charlotte's motherly instinct sharply kicked in; her own pain temporarily forgotten as she now had newfound hope. Holding Hannah in her arms, she replied, "Now, don't worry. Everything will be okay. We have a lot to catch up on before the little one is born."

Hannah smiled at Charlotte and gave her a hug. Charlotte and Hannah headed to the wake, leaving Sean to rest.

Sean could not believe it; he was going to be a father. But he himself had taken his chance of becoming a father away.

Thinking out loud Sean said, "That night I had a choice. Carry a knife or not. I did not need to carry a knife; I had never carried one before. But instead, I allowed what the media was reporting and social pressures to get inside my head and make me feel unsafe. Forcing me to do something I did not need to do.

I had no intention of using the knife that night, I should have left it at home with the negative energy. But instead, I am gone. My dreams can't be forced, my future finished before it began. And to top it off I cannot hold my own child, I cannot protect it, I cannot be called Daddy. Countless lives ruined from one stupid mistake. If there ever was a next time...there wouldn't be a next time. Think twice."

TWELVE

WITH PAIN COMES STRENGTH

Kelly had gotten used to life without Andrew quite quickly, the last two weeks felt like years. She was free, like a butterfly flying through a picturesque view on a sunny spring day. She was able to have fun again, laugh and enjoy life. Unfortunately, there was still something that brought her moments of joys to a prompt end. It was like a flu she could not shake. No matter how much sleep, water, or medication, it did not help, it made her ill.

Keeping the secret of Andrew murdering Sean was actually the easy part, it was having a secret which was harder. Every time Hannah mentioned Sean, or asked about becoming a parent, it hurt Kelly, so bad, it tore through her heart like a tiger's claw. But she had managed to keep strong and stick to her plan. Kelly knew one day soon it would be the right time to tell her daughter the truth.

The same day Kelly found out about Hannah, Sean, and the baby, she contacted DCI Summers to inform her of the change of events. As her commitment to her grandchild, Kelly promised to do all she could to make things right. The first matter was to make sure Andrew got the justice he deserved. Kelly went back to the station and on record told DCI Summers everything: every time Andrew struck and threatened her, even going as far as to bring doctors notes from all of the assaults. Although DCI Summers could not promise Kelly's fate, she was able to add two additional charges of grievous bodily harm against Andrew.

Kelly kept in touch with Andrew during his time on remand. He would call every day at 7 pm on the dot. Kelly made sure she answered as she did not want to raise any suspicion. The odd time Hannah would be in and they would have a little chat, Andrew having to make up what work he had been doing. Kelly told Hannah not to mention her pregnancy to her father until they were face to face as she did not want Andrew's poisonous ways to get into Hannah's head.

The conversations were difficult for Kelly, Andrew was very threatening towards her, implying that if she did not speak, he would get away with it. She often found herself cowering in a corner while on the phone. Andrew's reach was far.

There was little talk of Kelly, her feelings, even their home. All the time, he went on discussing legal matters. Naturally, it fell to Kelly to assist the barristers on Andrew's case, collecting personal statements and travelling to meetings. She referred to any money paid to his barristers as blood money. They knew he committed such a horrific crime, yet they were trying to keep his imprisonment to a minimum in exchange for money. The blood of Sean should stain their hands forever and even the best of deeds should not allow it to be washed away. The thought made her sick to her stomach, she did not see his barristers as humans from then on.

Time had passed by like a bus missing its stop, it was now time for Kelly to return to the police station to answer bail. She had not slept for four days prior to this, her over-thinking mind continuously produced a vivid scene every time she went to sleep: Kelly sat in a dark gloomy room, that had an unwelcoming stench, like a damp cellar. The walls were in disrepair, big chunks missing, paint peeling and mould growing in the corners.

Directly in front of Kelly was the judge, an aged man sat on his raised podium. He was so skinny you could see all the bones in his face. His teeth were black and as rotten as an old apple. His eyes bulged with anger, the white of his eyes red and the iris the darkest of black. With no facial hair, his bushy eyebrows stood out like caterpillars walking across a branch. His once black robe was grey, covered in cobwebs and dandruff. His bench wig was matted, it looked more like a sheep, with cock-roaches weaving in and out.

To the rear, left, and right of Kelly were the jurors, all as pale as ghosts with black bags underneath their eyes and scowling at her. The room was freezing cold, so cold, she could see her breath. She wanted to hug herself to keep warm, but her arm was tied behind her back. Goosebumps rose on her arms as her teeth chattered.

Taking Kelly's breath, the judge roared, "Did you kill that young boy?".

Her hair was blown back, as the chair tilted back on its rear legs from the force. Tipping forwards again, Kelly screamed, "No, it was not me".

The jurors leaned in closer, snarling at Kelly as the judge replied, "Lies, jurors, take a moment to view this memory."

The judge extended his arm from behind his raised desk and put his hand into Kelly's head. After rummaging around her mind like he was trying to find his favourite chocolate in a variety box, he dragged a memory out, causing Kelly excruciating pain.

A holographic memory played of Sean laying there, with blood gushing out of his neck, pleading for help. Kelly looking down at her blood-soaked hands and running off, leaving Sean there to die. The jurors leaned in closer to Kelly, they were so close she could feel their breath. They began to chant 'kill-er, kill-er, kill-er'. With each chant, the judge and the jurors grew larger, staring down on Kelly. She screamed as loud as she could that it was not the full memory. There was more to it and the important section was missing. The judge and jurors had spoken, the judge yelled, 'guilty'.

As the gavel hit the stand, the floor broke and Kelly fell. Falling deeper and deeper underground, something stopped her fall. It was dark. She rummaged around for a lighter. She found one and flicked it on. There was Sean, dead with a wide gouge in his neck.

He turned to Kelly and said, "You did this to me".

His mouth was moving but his eyes closed. In horror Kelly looked around, she was in Sean's casket, she attempted to climb out but could not. The judge and the jurors peered into the hole still chanting, 'kill-er'. The dirt poured over her as her fingernails clawed against the wall.

Let me out, she pleaded.

The level was rising, covering her mouth and she found it difficult to breathe. Just as the last handful was thrown, she shot up out of her sleep, shaking with cold sweats.

Later that day Kelly arrived at the police station, her stomach in knots. This could be last time she was free for a very, very long time. She wasn't waiting in reception for long before DCI Summers came to collect her. Following Summers along to the interrogation room, Kelly did not feel any calmer about the situation.

Opening the door with her knee and pushing it with her bum as her hands were full, Summers welcomed Kelly to enter the room. This time Kelly was able to feel the stillness of the room, the eeriness, the guilt from her last visit. Once sat at the table, Summers threw her files across it, scattering like a pack of cards.

Click. The recorder on again. Just for clarification, Summers asked for the version of events from that night. Not only did Kelly's versions match the events of everyone else, she now said on tape that her husband killed Sean, with a cold heart. Kelly also wanted to press charges for the assault on herself that night. Summers smiled and asked about the other accounts of grievous bodily harm, Kelly put them all on record.

"Kelly, the information you have given us is very important for our case. I have looked at the evidence for that night, along with your previous statements and looked at your doctor's notes. I am happy to release you without charge as you were not the one to blame for any incidents that occurred. I strongly believe that you would have helped Sean if you were not so scared of your husband. You have suffered domestic abuse for too long, Kelly. But it is over."

Tears of joy creeped out of Kelly's eyes. Thanking Summers for her support, Kelly got up and gave her a hug. Holding on, Summers told Kelly to be strong for Hannah and her grandchild, as they all had a very long road ahead of them.

Before leaving, Summers warned Kelly that she was going to inform Andrew's barristers about the additional chargers, giving time for Kelly to work out what she was going to do.

Kelly paused. "How long could Andrew get?"

Summers replied, "A very long time. Potentially, five years for each charge of grievous bodily harm on you, six months for the criminal damage at the restaurant and finally for the murder of Sean, we will aim for thirty years. So, forty-five years, give or take if he is found guilty".

Kelly nodded her head. Noticing what Kelly was doing as she often did it when calculating maths, Summers said, "Yes, he will most likely die behind bars, and if not, he will be an old man by the end of his sentence".

Stepping out of the station, Kelly felt like a huge weight had been lifted from her shoulders. Tilting her head to the sky, she sighed a sigh of relief. Ahhhhh, she breathed.

The blanket of depression hovering over Kelly since Sean's death broke and the sun rays beamed through, warming her face. The sky was the bluest of blue, grass the greenest of greens, colour flooded back to Kelly's vision. The air smelled different, even her taste buds started to tingle from the aroma coming from a takeaway across the road.

Kelly headed to the shopping mall for some clothes and refreshments then when back home to complete the rest of the plan. She waited by the phone, patiently twiddling her thumbs. Oddly enough, she was quite excited. All those years of fear, being bullied and intimidated were over and the one responsible for it would soon feel the workings of karma.

The phone rang, Kelly's heart started to beat faster, taking a deep breath so her heartbeat normalised. She answered the phone with a 'hello' but Andrew interrupted her immediately. He started by demanding she ring his barrister as he had not had any contact in weeks and the court date was now only a week away. He then proceeded to threaten Kelly to keep her mouth closed or he would make her life hell when he returned.

"You already made my life hell, Andrew. Every day for the past ten years, I have hated the sight of you."

"I'm only playing with you Kelly. I just want to get home so we can be a family again." Andrew could tell Kelly was being serious. But he continued "Me, you and Hannah. Back to how things were."

The other side of the line was silent. Andrew grew worried and made another attempt to win her back. "I'll even treat you to them fancy earrings that everyone is wearing."

"Andrew, that will not work anymore, your gifts cannot keep me quiet any longer. Everything you have ever got me was for you, not me. You killed that poor, young boy on purpose, you evil man."

"Kelly, what the hell are you playing at, saying that over the phone. Are you an idiot? You'll have me rotting in here, you stupid woman."

"No, Andrew I will not shut up anymore. I have told the police everything. Including the times you beat me black and blue when you hadn't had a fix."

Andrew was doomed, he no longer had a grip over his wife, so he used his last weapon in his arsenal to try and get her back under control, "What do you mean? Are you trying to keep me away forever, what about Hannah?"

Kelly hissed, "Don't you bring Hannah into your mess. Your web of lies, you make me sick. And to think Hannah will want anything to do with you after all this, don't make me laugh".

"Of course, she will, you deluded woman. I'm her dad. She'll understand that I acted in self-defence, the crazy boy was going to kill me," Andrew said in a smug fashion.

"Oh, about that. The boy, Sean, who you murdered. He was Hannah's boyfriend, the two were expecting a baby."

Andrew did not reply.

"That's what I thought Andrew, lost for words. You did not have to do what you did but you always have to be the big man, now look.

Expect to receive the news from your barristers tomorrow morning and do not bother me again." Kelly slammed down the phone before Andrew could answer, she was done.

Later that evening, Hannah returned home from a meal with her friends. Kelly was sat in the living room waiting for her. Hannah entered the room and sat in the leather single-seated chair as she always did.

"Have you heard from Dad?" she asked her mother.

"Love, I am not willing to protect him any longer. He must be held responsible for what he has done. Hannah, it was your father that killed Sean."

"What?" Hannah replied, having to cough to clear her throat.

Moving to the edge of her seat, Kelly told Hannah everything that happened that night and how she had suffered from domestic abuse for so long. There were tears, raised voices, conquered fears, and wrong choices but Kelly got it all off her chest. The most difficult part was explaining to her daughter how and why she kept it from her.

Truth be told, Hannah was quite understanding in the end. She understood why her mother did what she did, she just wanted to protect her. Hannah opened up about her dad's behaviour, informing her mum about the amount of times she heard him hit her too. She did not tell anyone because she did not want to make it worse for her mother.

Kelly was upset that she put so much on Hannah when she was trying to keep her safe. They both made an agreement never to talk to him or any man that acted like him again.

"Hannah, I've been thinking. We should invite Charlotte around so I can tell her exactly what happened that night."

"But Mum, what happens if she takes it out on you?"

"She will find out who I am sooner or later, and I would prefer it to come from me."

"Okay, I think we should do it."

"Can you arrange for tomorrow evening?"

Hannah agreed, as she went upstairs to get her phone.

Sitting at the table was Kelly, Hannah, and Charlotte. Kelly, with her new found confidence stepped up to lead the conversation. She began by telling Charlotte and Hannah that the purpose of the talk was to clear the slate for the future of the baby. Hannah and

Charlotte both nodding their head in agreement.

As expected, Charlotte was devastated to find out that it was Hannah's father who had murdered her son. At first, she had nothing but anger towards Kelly, feeling she could have done more to save him. The pain in Charlotte's heart was persistent, the only time it eased up was when she thought about providing some sort of justice for her son. In Charlotte's current broken state of mind, the only justice was to inflict serious harm to Kelly. She felt she was all out of options and revenge was the only way. *This woman is the reason my son is dead,* she thought.

Kelly anticipated that Charlotte would hold some hostility towards her, it became apparent through the piercing looks and nasty words.

She stood up for herself by saying, "Charlotte, I did all I could. That should not have happened to your son. But you know your son should not have had that knife either."

Charlotte was furious, how dare she talk about her dead son like that. She was ready to spit venom back at Kelly, but then Hannah laid her hand over hers. They all looked down at her bump, Charlotte realising it only hurt because it was the truth. The storm settled as they talk continued, clearing the canvas for the painting of what kind of a horrible, evil man Andrew was.

The closeness of the awkward atmosphere had evaporated. The three of them were making plans for the baby. Although, each of them recognised that part of them was taken away when Sean passed and it could not be filled. However, the baby gave each person at that table an opportunity to try to make things right. The conversation closed with Kelly asking Charlotte if Hannah could sit with her in court while she was giving evidence against her husband. Charlotte agreed then kissed them both on the cheek and gave them a hug before she left the house.

THIRTEEN

JUSTICE SERVED

The courtroom was larger than that in Kelly's nightmare but just as intimidating. At the front was a raised platform for the judge and directly in front was a table for the clerk, both areas facing the court. Facing the clerk were two tables, one for the defendant's team with a plastic box for the defendant, and the other for the prosecution.

Next to the defending barrister, positioned across the wall were seats for the jurors and opposite them the witness box. Finally, behind the barristers was a space for the public to sit. The public seating was split in two, to create an aisle for people needing access to the court.

The carpet was burgundy as were all of the seats. All tables were oak, matching the doors. The wall was oak too, up to about two-thirds of the height of the wall. The remaining third was painted white, as was the roof. A great big coat of arms sat behind the judge. It had a gold lion and a white unicorn holding a shield. The shield was split into four, one section had a red lion, two adjacent sections had three lions, and the fourth had a harp. Underneath the coat of arms read 'DIEU ET MON DROIT' which translates to 'God and my right'.

To reduce any risk of violence, people entered the court in a very strategic way. The jury and the clerk came in through a door to the top left of the room. The defence and Andrew came in from a door on the top left. And the prosecution, Hannah, Charlotte, and Sean's family and friends arrived through the double doors from the main entrance. The double door staying ajar while Sean's family and friends flooded in, occupying all of the seats.

The door on the top left opened and the judge walked out.

"All rise," the clerk said, as the judge proceeded to sit down. Once his behind was planted on the seat, the clerk spouted, "Be seated".

The judge was quite a heavyset man, with his stomach protruding from his bench gown. His

144

bench wig was combed to excellence, not a single strand was out of place. He had rosy red cheeks that sat perfectly above his neatly groomed beard. It was plain to see that the judge took pride in his appearance and his job.

Hannah looked over at her dad. With his over-grown hair and haggard face, he looked home-less. He had lost a lot of weight, the grey prison-issued jogging bottoms and jumper hung from him. Not one part of Hannah felt sorry for him. At home he was a bully but now look at him, a scared man, looking at the floor in shame.

The judge asked him his name, he answered, and the trial went on. The judge read a quick summary of what happened the night of Sean's death and the additional charges against him made by Kelly. There were tears, a lot of tears, but there was a mix of emotions from the public gallery. Some were sad to hear first-hand what had happened to Sean, while others were full of rage that his murderer was almost within arm's reach.

The judge asked Andrew whether he was guilty or not guilty of murder, three charges of grievous bodily harm and criminal damage.

Andrew replied, "Not guilty".

The crowd went into an uproar. Some people hurled threats at Andrew. The security was called and swiftly acted upon the brash behaviour, bringing it to an abrupt end when the aggressive ones were removed from the courtroom.

The game began, Andrew's point of defence was that he did not go out with a knife that night. Therefore, he did not mean to kill him. The witnesses were called to give their version of events, all enlightening the fact that Sean was only helping and posed no further threat to Andrew once he hit him.

The last witness to be called up was Kelly. As soon as she stepped into the stand, Andrew looked over and shouted abuse at her. The judge ordered him to stop. Not quite expecting that to happen, Kelly's emotions got the best of her. But she wiped away her tears, looked Andrew dead in the eye and told him that she was no longer afraid of him.

Informing the court what happened that night, emphasising that Andrew had no need to stab Sean, other than to make himself feel better. She also added that she could have helped Sean if Andrew did not force her to leave by dragging her away.

To build up a better case around Andrew, the prosecution also asked about his behaviour at the time of any other assaults on her, to which she told them about the years she had been subject to domestic abuse at the hands of her husband.

Unfortunately, the protection could not go into too much detail as it was unrelated to that case. Upon Kelly's completion of answering questions, the defence made one last attempt to try and sway the jury their way. The court closed for one hour for the jury to come to their verdict.

Most went to the canteen, it was an old school canteen, the type that smelt of frazzled bacon, burning the back of your throat as you entered. The seats were plastic and scratched across the floor, leaving black marks when moved. A group in the far-right corner of the canteen were having a debate on what happened, weighing up what was said and casting their own verdict. While others flicked through their phones, catching up on their news feed, Charlotte and Hannah had a cup of tea and went to the toilet.

On the way back to the canteen, Charlotte saw the two that been thrown out of court. She went straight to them to give them an earful and asked that they respect her son. Tension was high, people were snapping at each other. Eventually, the clerk came and welcomed them all back into the courtroom.

Once seated, the judge spoke, "Ladies and gentlemen of the court, we would like to thank you for your cooperation throughout this complex case." He nodded at the jury, "How do you find the accused?"

The foreperson of the jury stood up. "We find Mr Andrew Blacks guilty of criminal damage, guilty on one count of grievous bodily harm to Mrs Blacks and finally...", the court went silent, so silent the footsteps of people upstairs could be heard. "Guilty of the murder of Sean Barkly."

The crowd cheered and hugged one another. The defence waited until the cheers had stopped before delivering their statement of mitigation, asking for leniency as Mr Blacks is a successful businessman and this was his first serious offence. The judge thanked the jury, and turned to Andrew to deliver his sentencing.

"Mr Blacks, you will serve six months and a £1500 fine for the criminal damage caused at the restaurant. A further five years for the grievous bodily harm caused to your wife on the same night. Now, Mr Blacks, please do not feel you have gotten away with the two other accounts of grievous bodily harm, because this is far from the truth. There is no doubt in my mind, you have caused harm to your wife plenty of times before, but on this occasion, there was not enough evidence to prove you did. It does not, by any stretch of the imagination make you any less of a bully."

"Mr Blacks, you had a choice that night. But as your ego was damaged, you chose to stab Mr Barkly while he was helping your wife. You are no man Mr Blacks; you are in fact, a coward. I sentence you to life imprisonment, in total, thirty-six years in jail."

The judge slammed the gavel down. "As I believe you would do this again, I consider you a risk to the public and therefore are classed as a danger to life. Furthermore, you will be given imprisonment for public protection, meaning after you have served your thirty-six years, you will not smell freedom until the parole board assesses you as suitable."

The judge turned to the public and gave them a word of warning in an exceedingly stern tone, "Although justice has been served here, let this be a stark reminder of what can happen if you choose to carry a knife. The possibility of you either facing a judge or facing your maker is high. Don't waste your life, there is always an alternative."

FOURTEEN

CAGED ANIMAL

Andrew was remanded for the murder of Sean and sent straight to prison until his court date. While on remand, he had thought he was going to get away with it, showing the full extent of his naivety.

The prison where he spent his time before his court case was a new build, so everything in there was new. His room was no different to a low budget hotel room, just a touch smaller. Looking in from the door on the right was a toilet and sink, then a bed with a white cover. On the back wall, facing the door was a thin strip of a window, no wider than eight inches that looked out over the exercise area. On the left of the room, was a desk with a plastic chair shoved neatly underneath. Connected to that were drawers for storage.

Andrew paused to wonder why there were no wardrobes, blind to the fact that the rail could be made into a deadly weapon. The light bounced off the freshly painted walls, making the room look very bright. There was even a little TV, facing away from the door as if it were too shy to talk.

There were no rules there, the inmates went in and out of the cells as they wished, they met up to play board games as and when. There were rarely any fights, the only time when tensions rose was when an inmate had cheated at a board game. But this type of attention brought the prison officers around.

They would simply ask, 'You don't want me to report this do you?'

The commotion would soon calm back down. Nothing like you see on a TV series. After all, this was not really seen as a prison, just a big holding facility. The hardest part for Andrew was not having access to drugs, but this hardship was not for long as he soon got them in the palm of his hands.

Funnily enough, Andrew was introduced to his barristers through his dealer. So, when he was on the inside, he still had contact with him. He was able to get payment to his dealer on the outside, through his corrupt barristers, something that Kelly knew nothing about. The transaction was simple, she paid them, they paid the dealer, who in turn told his associate on the inside that it was okay to give Andrew the goods. It had to happen this way as all payments in this new jail were electronic. Meaning there was no cash, as any cash would be confiscated.

Andrew was no fool, he knew his stay there was temporary, as inmates went to court and never came back. But him not coming back, meant that he was free. That was until he received the news from Kelly. Everything went downhill from that moment. With no access to the barristers, Andrew's drug supply came to a jolting halt. Consequently, his anger increased as his temper decreased.

After days and days of begging with his contact to lend him the drugs, he grew impatient. Andrew approached him in the library, pleading again.

However, on this occasion, the dealer stood in Andrew's face and said, "Look, if you haven't got the money, you do not get the gear. Now move yourself from me, before I make sure you never talk to me again".

Andrew felt the anger in him rise from his feet. His fist clenched, face screwed, and teeth snarled. Andrew felt he was going to explode, he picked up the nearest object, a heavy book and struck the dealer. Bang, the sound of the connection echoed throughout the small library catching the attention of the guards. By the time they arrived, the dealer was laid out on the floor and Andrew was leaning over him attempting to pummel his face beyond recognition.

With no warning, a guard struck Andrew on the back of the neck with his baton knocking him unconscious. Andrew fell in a heap and was dragged to solitary confinement while asleep like a baby. Fortunately for Andrew, the dealer told the guards they had a dispute over football teams and did not want to press charges.

From that day until the court date, Andrew stayed in that solitary room. No shower, no conversations, no phone calls. Just him, his own thoughts, and drug withdrawals. The first nights were the worst, he would sweat profusely but was shivering like he was sat in a freezer. The shivering caused the whole of his body to ache as if he had been to the gym. He would often hallucinate that four-year-old

Hannah was with him in the pit. He would play for hours on end.

Coming out of solitary clean from drugs, he still blamed everyone else for his predicament, showing no remorse for murdering Sean. One thing for sure was that he missed his daughter dearly, at night he was often brought to tears. Not because of what he did, or because of what he had put her through, but because he missed his beautiful daughter and was sure she would feel the same.

After court had finished, Andrew was put in the back of the transportation van. His next stop, prison, where he will more than likely be until his death. Getting banged about in the back of the van brought Andrew back to his senses. At first, he could not remember where he was. He was dazed, confused, like a hare in headlights. But then his memory came back, hitting him like a bat to a ball.

The sound of the gavel crashing down on the stand stuck in the forefront of his mind, going over and over. The gavel did not only crash onto the stand that day, but it crashed down on Andrew's whole life as well.

Pulling up to the external entrance of the prison, Andrew glanced out of the window. For as long as he could see, there was a twelve-foot metal fence topped with razor-sharp barbed wire. Turning away, without having to see the prison building, Andrew knew straight away that this prison was not the same as the one he was previously staying in; this prison was serious.

The brakes of the van squealed like a toy being pressed too hard as it pulled up to the main arrivals entrance. He could hear the driver and the guard talking but could not make out what was being discussed. Everything was muffled inside the well-insulated box. The door at the rear caused the van to rattle as it was opened. Each time the door of a box was opened, Andrew could hear the jangle of keys and footsteps out of the van. He knew when a prisoner departed the van, it would jump up. 'Click', Andrew's door opened, standing before him was a big chap, with a big beard and hairy arms, looking like a bear.

Staring Andrew in the face, the guard said, "C'mon, you're home."

He opened the door for Andrew to get out. The guard allowed Andrew to go first as there was another guard waiting at the rear of the van. Andrew ducked down as he walked out, then jumped on the floor to be escorted to the booking-in bay.

On the way across, Andrew took his first look at his new home. It was huge, like a castle. He looked up as far as his neck allowed but the building still went up. Built with stone, it had four watch towers, one at each corner. Every window was covered with thick steel bars, some had white sheets hanging from them. It was dark and gloomy; it would have looked well placed in a horror film.

"Home," Andrew muttered under his breath.

His experience of the booking-in was not too bad. Andrew just had to confirm his name and in return he was given a bag of necessities to get him started: toothbrush, toothpaste, soap, deodorant, and a fresh burgundy jogging suit. There were no jokes, no banter, everyone was serious. The atmosphere was nothing like the previous place. It was extremely tense, like anything could happen at any time; no holds barred.

Andrew waited for his medical with the rest of the prisoners that were in the van with him. While waiting he assessed the other inmates, paying attention to their face and hands. This was the first time Andrew had witnessed such rough looking people in the same room. Scars, signs of broken bones, they should all come with warning signs.

Andrew was called in for his medical and asked a series of questions; Do you have any health conditions? Do you suffer from mental health issues? Do you suffer from substance misuse?

Do you feel you might hurt yourself? All were answered with a 'no'. The final question went, "What are you here for Mr Blacks?" the nurse asked.

"Assault," said Andrew.

There was an awkward pause, the nurse prompted for the other charges. Andrew had forgotten that Sean had died.

"Mr Blacks you are here for murder, grievous bodily harm, and criminal damage."

Andrew hung his head in shame.

"Mr Blacks, it is not my place to say so, but those charges are very serious. I have seen thousands of prisoners in my time and you don't strike me as a serious one. Listen. Women beating, child murders are frowned upon in here, so if I were you, I would keep that little secret to yourself," advised the nurse.

Andrew thanked her.

"Don't thank me. I'm not doing it for you, this prison does not need any extra trouble."

A prison guard took Andrew to his cell, he made no attempt to make Andrew feel welcome. It was although the guard knew what he had done: the nurse was not trying to intimidate him; she was warning him.

Coming out, the smell hit Andrew first. He could not put his finger on the smell itself, but its link was very strong to the smell of his old primary school. It looked awful, it was very plain and unhomely, there were rows of huge iron bars all over.

At the beginning and the end of each wing was a spiral staircase that went from the ground floor all the way up to the top floor like a helter-skelter. At each level, the staircase housed a door to gain access to that floor.

The bottom floor was split into two halves like a football pitch, the first half had offices on the right and a kitchen on the left, the second half was outlined in cells. A table tennis board and a pool table were placed in the second half, allowing inmates easy access to play.

Separating the two sections was a wall of thick iron bars with a heavy door between the two sections for access. In the middle of the iron wall was a metal staircase leading to the next floor.

The remaining levels had cells around the outside with a meter-wide walkway. On the upper levels, there were walkways leading to the staircase. Nets were placed in the huge gaps to prevent prisoners from jumping off or being thrown off.

During the journey to his cell Andrew did not see many people, only the odd cleaner and prison guard. Arriving at his new pad, the prison guard opened the door and walked off.

The layout was similar to the one on the previous jail. However, this one was only twelve by eight feet and the ceiling was very low. There were bunk beds in place of the single bed. It was freezing, the cold catching the back of Andrew's throat, causing him to cough. The walls were stone and covered in magnolia paint, with the additional splatter of blood from a fight or where a drug addict had injected maybe?

Andrew threw his clear plastic bag of belongings on the side and laid on the bottom bunk to collect his thoughts, he did not even bother to remove his shoes. The stress of the day had made him tired. So he stepped on the lower bunk to push himself up the ladders to the empty top bunk and drifted off.

He was woken up out of his sleep by his feet getting slapped off the bed. Andrew jumped like he had a drink spilt on him. He was still half-asleep while being dragged from his bed. It was only when he hit the floor that he woke up.

"What do you think you're doing?" he shouted, as he scrummaged to his feet.

The inmate did not respond, he just looked at him.

Andrew shouted again, "C'mon, what do you think you are doing?"

Andrew approached him, then stopped around four inches away from the other inmate.

Crash, the man leapt forward with his head, causing it to crush against Andrew's nose, bending it like a nail that had not been hit from the correct angle. His nose started pouring with blood instantly. He used both his hands to try and stop the blood from going every-where.

"That was your moving in present, my friend. I'm your cellmate. I would appreciate it if you didn't put your dirty trainers on my bed." The inmate responded with a smirk.

Using his towel to mop up his blood, Andrew was livid. But what could he do? This was his first day inside and judging by what the nurse advised, he could not afford to draw any more attention to himself.

Andrew did not sleep a wink, there were peo-ple shouting and banging on doors. His tired-ness brought on paranoia, thinking that the in-mates were sending him death threats. The morning soon approached, his cellmate went to the toilet and saw him awake.

"Morning mate, guessing you didn't sleep much."

Andrew's nose was still in pain and although his predicament could not contain violence, he definitely did not want to talk to this man. Picking up on the atmosphere he spoke again.

"Listen mate, last night. Stuff happens, you came into the cell with total disregard and disrespected your cellmate. Now, if someone else was your cellmate, that may not have happened. But on the contrary, you could have had your head bounced off every wall in the cell. Anyway, you have a choice here; You can either fight me for the bottom bunk or take it as a lesson learned. And before you make your decision, remember you are new here and I am the only person you have met. So, it is totally up to you?"

Andrew's arm was literally twisted behind his back, he had no other option but to swallow his pride, for now. Knowing he had no other option, Andrew introduced himself, putting his hand over the edge of the bed to shake his cellmate's hand.

"They call me Sy, short for Simon," he replied as he shook Andrew's hand.

For breakfast, the pool tables were pushed to the edge and portable benches were put out in their place. Each level was allowed thirty minutes to eat their meal, once one level had gone back into their cells, another level was able to go and eat. The door opened; it was breakfast time for Andrew's level. He and Sy headed down. Just as they were about to reach the stairs, Sy noticed Andrew did not have his plastic cup and turned to him.

"Mate, where's your cup, you need it for a drink, did you get it out of your bag?"

Andrew shook his head and ran back for the plastic cup. Scurrying through his stuff like a squirrel for a nut Andrew found the cup and turned to head back down for breakfast. Just as he was about to exit the room, three inmates entered.

One of them asking, "New boy, what have you got?"

"What are you on about?" Andrew replied.

Two of the inmates grabbed Andrew by the arms and shoved him against the wall, while the other inserted a black sock in Andrew's mouth to stop him from shouting. The third inmate searched the room high and low, making sure Sy's things went untouched, nothing.

One of the others pulled down Andrew's trousers exposing his genitals. The third inmate took a swing at Andrew's testicles. His eyes streamed with tears as he let out a muffled scream due to the excruciating pain. The third inmate checked to see if anything had fallen out of Andrew's rear, it did not. The three inmates left Andrew in a ball on the floor, cupping his groin in pain.

Sy returned to the cell before Andrew had a chance to get up. Spotting Andrew on the floor, he asked, "What the hell happened to you, mate?"

Andrew told him what had just happened.

"Oh, they were after illegal contraband: phones, drugs or money. When people come in, they sometimes bring it inside their rear. That's what they were checking. If you had anything up there, it would have found its way out when they hit you."

Not even twenty-four hours inside and Andrew had already been exposed to the receiving end of violence, more than he had ever endured. It could only get better right?

FIFTEEN

THE MAN, THE MYTH, THE LEGEND

Andrew found it hard to adapt to his new life: one shower a week, limited time out of his cell or outside in the fresh air, and living with a stranger. But the thing he found the hardest to adapt to was the lack of control he had. On the outside, Andrew controlled everything; when he worked, what he wore, where he went, what his wife wore, the list went on. However, in here he could make one choice; what he was having to eat.

Finding it hard to gel with the other inmates, Andrew became reclusive, not leaving his cell much, only for food and showers. With his success outside, he felt that he was somehow above the other inmates. He did not class himself as a criminal and found it impossible to differentiate the world on the inside from the world on the outside. On the outside, the law was governed by professions, inside the law is governed by the inmates.

He was scared, he did not know who to trust. Sy introduced him to a few other inmates but Andrew was not keen on them, so he kept his distance. Andrew did notice one thing though, the inmates that lived nicely were the ones that had an income, largely from handling illegal goods or intimidation.

Andrew had never done anything of the sort, and he was not going to start now. He found it disgusting living alongside people who participated in such actions. His only option was to keep his head low and take each day as it came. Unfortunately for him, this approach was due to take a drastic transformation.

One afternoon, Andrew was sat at the bench munching on his food when he received a huge slap on the back. The sound attracted the attention of the inmates around the table, they all looked over as soon as they realised who it was. The culprit walked around the table and pushed an inmate from his seat so he could sit directly across from Andrew.

"What's good, family?" the man said.

"I think you have the wrong person," Andrew replied.

"Oh, so we're not family now, no?" the man asked.

Andrew ignored him, he could not see this conversation going very far. He genuinely thought the man was talking to the wrong person.

The man became exaggerated in his actions, grabbing inmates next to him for support, acting like he was upset that Andrew did not recognise him as his family. Looking like something from a comedy sketch, the man turned to Andrew.

"So, if my little brother was having a child to your daughter, doesn't that basically make us family?"

The colour drained from Andrew's face, his secret exposed. This man knew who he was. Looking around the table to see if any inmates were listening, they all looked away as if they were not paying attention. The man's exaggerated gestures promptly turned into aggression, throwing the plate of food at Andrew.

"My little brother cannot see his child. Why is that Mr Andrew Blacks?"

Andrew froze, the words of warning from the nurse echoing in his head. He opened his mouth to reply but no words came out on his first attempt. Clearing his throat, Andrew took a second attempt, looking down.

"I killed him."

"You what, you killed my little brother," the man said, in a sarcastic voice.

Andrew stayed silent.

"Did you not hear me, why did you kill my little brother?"

Andrew took a deep breath. "Because he stopped me from hitting my wife."

When hitting his wife, Andrew had felt empowered, but when he said it out loud now, he felt ashamed. Accidentally breaking the tension, an inmate knocked his plastic cup over. It bounced like a ball before rolling down to the end of the bench. The man did not respond verbally, instead picking up the cup and placed it in front of Andrew.

Michael then reached towards Andrew, grabbing his head with both hands like a basketball. With his hands gripped firmly, he rammed Andrew's head onto the cup. Thud, blood splattered everywhere like it was water rinsing off a spoon. He licked the blood from his forearm while walking off. Blood trickled out of the huge gash on Andrew's forehead, covering his face.

"Don't rest, you'll be hearing from me," he said. He chuckled loudly as he walked up the stairs.

The guards watched on as if it were business as usual. Not moving until the man had left, they approached Andrew.

The guard jested, "Wow fella, you went with a right bang. You need to be careful where you're walking".

Blood pouring from Andrew's head, he could not look up to answer the guard as it trickled into his eyes. Seeing the depth of the cut, the guards took Andrew to the medical room to get his head stitched up.

After a short visit to the medical room, Andrew returned to his cell. Upon his entry, Sy shot out of bed clenching his fists.

"You killed a young boy because he stopped you from hammering your wife. I should do you over right now. You mug."

Andrew responded, "It was in self-defence, the lad knocked me clean to the ground." And as for my wife, flirting with men when I took her out, the slag. What happens between me and my wife is our business. I only ever hit her when she deserved it. All that I did for her, the clothes, the jewellery, the holidays, and she couldn't even show me respect. She was bang out of order."

"Listen you mug," Sy replied, "I don't care about your soppy story, playing the victim. A young lad is dead because he handled you and you couldn't take it. I know your type a mile off, just like my stepdad. I put him under, I'll put you under as well."

Both men heated, they each stood their ground. They were ready to fight for what they believed in. Andrew took a step back, ready to fight. Sy had already got him with a cheap shot on his first day, he was not going to let it happen again.

To Andrew's surprise, Sy turned around. Something was wrong, they were ready to go for it, Andrew wanted to settle his score. Sy punched the cupboard in front of him. Shaking his hand in pain, he told Andrew he was the luckiest, unlucky man on Earth.

"What are you talking about?" Andrew asked.

"The young boy you killed is the brother of the man who runs this prison, Big Juj. Saying that, it's not just this one, it is any prison that he goes to. You see how you have people who run the wing, he runs the people that run the wing. Oh, and he pretty much controls the prison guards as well. Have you noticed we're never in the same place as other inmates from another wing, apart from if we're passing? That is because each wing has their own part of the prison. Not Big Juj. He walks freely around the prison, in his prison like it is his home.

You don't get so much power from being a nice guy, this guy is evil. When I say evil, I mean he is so evil, he thinks that God is too weak. Therefore, he worships the Devil himself. He is well known for slaughtering people and smearing their blood all over himself, in order to possess more power from dark sources."

Sy could see the worry on Andrew's face. "I know he is crazy, some argue he has mental health issues, but I don't think so, he is very smart. He recognises exactly what he is doing. He knows a lot on how the brain works; neurolinguistics and has extensive knowledge of leaders and how they use fear to control the masses. He has utilised his knowledge and now has people that will do whatever he wants them to out of pure fear.

Now back to what I said earlier about you being a lucky and an unlucky man. You are lucky because I want to hurt you, but Big Juj has put a marker on you. So, nobody is allowed to lay a finger on you. So, I can't touch you luckily. However, you are unlucky because your life is now in the hands of a mad man."

Andrew asked himself why repeatedly, as he placed both of his hands against the wall along with his forehead, making sure he did not break his freshly stitched cut. Why did Sean have the knife? Why did it have to be the younger brother of this psychopath? Why did his wife have to make him angry? Pacing up and down his cell, Andrew questioned everything that had put him in his position. Imagine something putting the fear of God in you, then think how bad it would have to be to put the fear of the Devil in you.

It had been a few days since Andrew had heard from Big Juj. Things were different - nobody would acknowledge him, never mind talk to him. The only interactions were dirty looks and rude remarks muttered under the breath of the guards. During meal time, nobody would sit next to him. Sy would only talk to him in his cell at night. Andrew was now an outsider; he was all on his own and he knew it. Andrew flinched at every loud bang and every time someone shouted. He was living in fear.

Returning from lunch, Andrew was welcomed by a small parcel wrapped in newspaper on his bed. Upon closer inspection the words, K E E P T H I S O N Y O U were circled in red pen. The second he read the message, he looked around him to see who was looking. He then frantically shoved it in his pocket. It did not take him long to figure out who it was from.

Within the hour, an inmate approached Andrew and asked him, 'if he had it'. He went to retrieve the parcel from his pocket, then it dawned on him that the parcel said to keep it. Andrew played the fool, he responded like he did not know what the inmate was talking about. But it was too late, the inmate already saw him go into his pocket, he tried to grab his hand.

Andrew struck the man in the groin with his knee, forcing all the air out of his lungs. He then jumped up and elbowed him in the back of the head. The mad man dropped to the floor like a sack of rubbish, allowing Andrew to make a run for it.

Breathless, Andrew reached his cell. He went straight to the sink to splash his face with water, in the hope of waking him up from this bad dream. He dried off his face with a towel. Highlighting another thing Andrew disliked about prison, nothing was soft. Everything felt like it was washed with starch. To bring himself back to reality and to question his actions, Andrew looked at himself in the mirror. He was not the only person in the mirror staring back.

Clap, Clap, Clap. Big Juj clapped, congratulating Andrew while laughing. The depth of Big Juj's voice hit the pit of Andrew's stomach, giving him the shivers like someone stepped on his grave. He did not dare move, he just looked, and hoped. With his hands held back, Big Juj slowly bent down.

Lowering his mouth to Andrew's ear, he whispered, "Juju".

With that word, the air went blistering cold and Andrew struggled to breathe. The feeling left as did Big Juj.

A huge sigh of relief left Andrew's body. Gripping hold of the sink, his eyes were closed as he shook his head. He was just taking a moment to try and understand what he had got in to. Andrew did not leave his cell for the rest of the day, not even for food. He laid on his bed making pictures out of the cracks on the roof, like he and Hannah used to with clouds. It soon dawned on him that Big Juj would have a hold on him forever. Wondering what he had planned for him gave him nightmares.

Big Juj's control games did not end there. One night when Andrew was asleep and dreaming of being reunited with his family again, the guards raided his cell. Eight of them bounded in with riot helmets and shields. The guards ripped the cell apart, searching through every nook and cranny. They found the package. Everyone was in the shock when they saw pictures of one of the top ranking prison guard's wife in a rather compromising position with the best man at his wedding.

Andrew was thrown in to what was known as the hole. A dark circular room with a light at the top, like it was a well. He was thrown in so hard, he slipped on his back. Following him promptly was one of the guards, accompanied with a baton in his hand. He hit Andrew until he could not hold the baton up any longer. Andrew was beaten black and blue, his face looking like it had done ten rounds with Mike Tyson, with no gloves. While beating him, the guard was shouting.

"How did you get that?"

Andrew was adamant he was not going to say a word, but he was sure he was going to die. Just as he took what he thought was his last breath, he said it. "Big Juj".

Drip, Drip. Water from the window dropped on Andrew's face like a tap that was not turned off properly. Coming around slowly, he had forgotten where he was. He panicked and attempted to get up but was too sore from his injuries. He soon remembered where he was. He was alive, but for how long?

A guard checking up on Andrew, saw he was awake and informed him that he had been asleep for two days, showing the extent of his injuries. His sides hurt when he coughed, his chest hurt when he breathed, his eyes stung when he looked at the light. Karma for the times he had put his wife in that very position.

The next morning, Andrew was taken back to his cell. He begged the guards not to go back, he knew something bad was going to happen. The guards ignored his pleas. Arriving at his cell, he noticed it was still in the same state as he left it. Andrew grabbed a chair and sat down as he could not physically climb into his bed. Waiting for Sy, he dropped off.

The hairs on the back of Andrew's neck stood up, he heard it again, 'JUJU'. He opened his eyes and there before him was Big Juj.

"Yes family, why have I had the guards asking me about some strange package they took from your cell?" he asked.

Andrew did not bother to answer, they both knew why. Two additional inmates came into the cell. Big Juj turned to the left inmate, who was around six feet tall and weighed twenty stone. He nodded, doing the same to the other inmate on his right who was a little taller but just as heavy. Andrew knew that he was giving the inmates the green light. Big Juj walked out, closing the door behind him. The two inmates carried out their assault: they dragged him from his chair and bent him over it, tying his hands to the chair legs. Andrew attempted to fight back, but he was easily overpowered, he had no chance.

The inmates pulled down his bottoms, exposing his bum. One of the inmates got a light bulb out of his pocket and inserted it into Andrew's anus. The more Andrew wept, begging for them to stop, the further he pushed it in. The inmate would pull it out, like he had stopped and then insert it again. The other inmate laughed as he recorded it. Pausing the recording, the inmate holding the phone helped to bound Andrew's legs together. Andrew stood there with his bottom half-naked and a light bulb sticking out of his anus and arms tied in front of him, trying to cover his genitals. One of the inmates whispered in Andrew's ear.

"I wonder if your daughter knows how kinky you are. I bet she will when she sees the video on social media." Both of the inmates laughed, adding that if Andrew had a good idea the bulb may turn on.

Andrew was then prodded on his chest, causing him to lose balance. Falling backwards towards the chair, the worry on his face was clearly visible. As he landed on the chair, the bulb smashed. Andrew let out a yelp as he felt the glass tear through his skin. The damage wasn't invisible but the excruciating pain was there. As the blood trickled from the seat,

Andrew felt light-headed. He attempted to get up to seek help, but he fell forward, passing out on the floor with his head just poking out of the cell doorway.

Waking up in the prison hospital, Andrew was suffering mentally. The humiliation of the latest incident really hurt him and the fact they recorded it and were threatening to put it online for his daughter to see, he decided enough was enough.

During his time at the hospital, he wrote Hannah a letter in an bid to tell her everything she needed to know. After opening his heart in the letter, Andrew felt like a huge weight lift off his shoulders and decided it was time to take back control of his life. Returning to his pad, he noticed that all of Sys belongings were gone.

"Where is Sy, all his stuff has gone?" he asked a passing guard.

"He requested a move and it was granted."

Andrew did not have to ask why, he knew the answer as did the guard. Sat gingerly on the edge of his bed, he reflected on his life, Andrew was alone, not only on the inside but on the outside as well. His life no longer had meaning.

After the guards completed their last patrol before the shift change, he removed the stiff white bedsheet from his neatly laid bed. He then looped it around the top bar of the window and tied it so tight the bar almost submitted in pain. Wrapping the other half of the bedsheet around his neck, he took control back of his life. He leapt from his top bunk. At no point did Andrew struggle, like he had made a mistake and wanted to live.

"I'm sorry," he gasped with his last breath before his body started to twitch.

During the midnight patrol, his limp body was found hanging from the window. The guard called for backup and proceeded to take Andrew down, laying him on the hard ground.

Administering cardiopulmonary resuscitation (CPR), the guard's hands made Andrew's chest bend inwards as he pressed down on it. The manager arrived and knelt next to Andrew checking his pulse, nothing. He looked at the guard and shook his head, the guard stopped CRP. They covered him with the bedsheet. Andrew was gone.

SIXTEEN

WITH AN OPEN HEART

Dear Sweetie,

It's me, Dad. We have not had a proper conversation since I told you I was working away, even then it was only a quick hi and bye. I do not know where to start, so I will start right at the beginning, your birth. When me and your mum found out we were pregnant we were so happy, but scared. We didn't think we had enough money to bring another person into this world, but we wanted a family more than anything. So, I had to work harder in a factory to provide for you, like a father is supposed to. The day we found out you were a girl; I chose your name, Hannah. There was no sentimental reason for it, I just liked it as it can be spelt the same way forwards and backwards. Pretty cool, right? I did investigate the meaning a little deeper and found it was of Hebrew origin and that it means 'grace'. A grace is most certainly what you were.

You were such a cute little thing; I was in love with you from the second I first ever saw you. You did and still do brighten up my dark days. Your first word was 'Daddy', your mother was so annoyed haha. I'm delighted that I had the chance to see my little chubby cherub grow up into a beautiful, polite, young woman.

Bringing you up was very difficult for me and your mother. I worked every hour I could to provide, meaning I could hardly be with you guys, my family. While I worked, your mother looked after you. She went through a lot being a new mum all alone, but she did an excellent job - just look at you.

It became apparent that I could not work enough hours in that low paying factory job to give you or your mother the life you deserved.

So, I decided to set up my own plumbing business. This was only possible because of you. You gave me the drive, ambition, and motivation to do it.

The business took off quick, but with success came great responsibility. I found that by having total control, I could manage things better. This mindset for work ended up taking over my life. I had to have complete control over everything, apart from you, I could not tell you 'no'. Your mother was a different story, we often ended up fighting because she would not listen. I will be the first to admit it, I had some serious issues; I just needed a bit of time to fix them.

Your mother told me it was your boyfriend I murdered. But honestly Hannah, I did not know it was him. It all happened so fast. I did not carry that knife; you know how I feel about that. My stance was always to fight with fists. But I just lost it, everything went black. The next thing I knew, I was throwing a knife covered in blood on the ground and running away.

I am heartbroken, I have always dreamt of becoming a grandfather. Making up for the time I missed with you, I guess. Picking the little one up from nursery and school all the time. Taking you all on family holidays. Having everyone around the table for Christmas dinner. Me cutting the turkey in my Christmas jumper and party hat. But that can't happen, and I understand why. I have broken our family, the one thing I vowed to protect. And I will never be able to look in my grandchild's face knowing that I took his father's life.

Sweetie, I don't know what I can do for you to forgive me, I don't think you ever will. And I cannot even try to make things right from here. This is my mess and the only thing I can do from here is spare you any further shame and embarrassment. I'm sure your mum will look after you well and I don't blame you if you act like I never existed.

Love you forever,

Dad xxx

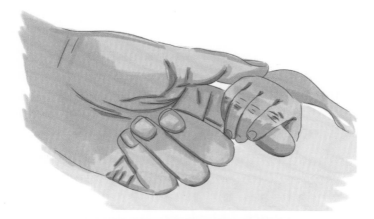

SEVENTEEN

A KING IS BORN

The day Andrew was sentenced, Hannah looked at her father differently. The man she saw in the courtroom was not her father but a weak, frail, scared, coward. He could not even look in the eyes of those whose lives he had torn apart, never mind apologise. He just sat there with his head down, like an ostrich burying its head in the sand. Like he did nothing wrong and he was just waiting for it all to blow over. All his trust in his barristers defending him, blaming everyone else for his cowardice actions.

When she saw her dad shout at her mum, it infuriated her immensely. All these people yelling abuse at him from the public seating area and he could not even look at them. But when his wife, the one he shared his life with, the person he trusted to have a child with, was in front of him, he attempted to bully her, to scare and intimidate her. It just summed up the horrible, controlling man he really was.

Kelly made Hannah so proud when she stood her ground. The pained look on her father's face when he saw his wife wipe her tears away and finally share her story. At that point, Andrew realised he no longer had control over her. What her mother did that day was not only for herself, but her actions should be used to empower all women going through domestic abuse to stand up and say no is no.

Seeing her father get sentenced to so many years in prison, knowing that he may never go home sparked off emotions like fireworks in Hannah's head. These emotions were not sad, or angry, but more disbelief than anything. If this was her father's true colours, then who was this man who had acted like he loved her? Who was this man that said he worked so hard to provide for her and her mum? This imposter. This fake. This fraud. She felt betrayed.

Hannah did not really get a chance to sit and think about the loss of Sean and the fact that it was her father that murdered him. Everyone was keeping her busy on purpose, with breaks away, shopping trips for the baby, arranging visitors and baby scans. However, if Hannah really wanted to, she could but fear was preventing her from doing so.

She was all too aware of the complexity of what had happened. The questions and answers weaved in and out like a messy bowl of spaghetti. The start could not be torn apart from the end and the mass of this mess was the middle.

At night, the part where you are tired but not quite ready to fall asleep was the hardest. That was the point where Hannah imagined times of life with Sean still there. Her and Sean would be looking for prams and other baby equipment. Him running around the store with a doll in the pram to make her laugh. She would have Sean going to parenting classes learning about becoming a new dad, often giggling at the faces he would have pulled. She imagined how they would sit and map out their future as a family. Their jobs, their first house, whether they would have a real or fake Christmas tree. Would they all have gone to America while Sean completed his placement or would they have stayed here? The world was their oyster. They would also have bets on what their child would want to be one day. Sean was the only person who made Hannah feel complete. But just as she was drifting off, reality would hit, Sean was gone. She would fall asleep with hope leaving her dreams, in the form of tears.

Hannah had zero contact with her father since she found out the horrid truth about him. She threw away the letter that he sent her before she even opened it. There was nothing he could have said to change it, he had single-handedly wrecked her life, turning it upside down and there was nothing that could be done to rectify it. She hated her dad, that was for sure, but this sort of hate was odd.

She knew all too well he had provided all the material things she ever wanted, to which she was grateful. But he had not really been there for her like her mum was. She felt like she could not tell her dad her feelings or worries or her thoughts. On reflection, Hannah noticed she did not have many memorable times with her dad, they were mostly with her mother. She now questioned if she loved him for being a father or because he was called her father.

She had noticed how her dad was so mean and nasty to her mum, but he was never like that with her. This made Hannah feel guilty as she knew her mum did not do anything other than her best. Stupid things Hannah would do, like, leave the milk out of the fridge or spill cereal on the side, would prompt her dad to barrage her mum with insults. It got the point that when Hannah knew her dad was coming home, she would leave the house. She did not like him being there.

Blaming her dad for the death of Sean, she also felt her mum could have done more. She had to tell her; she could not forgive until she did. When she woke the next morning, she dressed quickly and headed down to the kitchen. Grabbing her mum by the hand, Hannah pulled her over to sit down together.

"Mum I can't help it, but I feel like I partly blame you for what happened to Sean. I know what dad was like with you, and I know how he used to hit you. But it took someone to die for you to want to make a change. It was far too late. You should have left him way before that. I understand you thought you were protecting me. But Mum, it was not. It made me feel bad, like all your arguments were my fault, I hated it."

Kelly's head dropped while Hannah was speaking, she felt so ashamed, she couldn't even look her own daughter in the eyes. Her eyes filled up with tears, but she had no right to feel so sad while her daughter was being so strong. Not that Hannah said anything hurtful, but because Kelly thought she had failed as a parent. However, she now understood that hiding things that are wrong can be just as harmful as being honest.

As the baby bump grew, so did Hannah's worries about becoming a parent, especially so young. She had very little responsibility at home, did not have to cook, clean, or do the shopping. How on earth was she meant to support her child when she was so heavily supported herself? Doubt riddled through her body.

Luckily, Hannah was able to finish the year in college. Her grades were as predicted, despite all of the drama she went through. This was only possible because she made a promise to Sean, that she would follow her dream of becoming a vet.

Unfortunately, she missed out on going to university because of her pregnancy so she decided to take a gap year. Work-wise, Hannah never had a job as her parents said they would support her while in education. But with her dad gone, how would this be possible? Hannah presumed she would have to get a job shortly after the birth of her child. But she was ready, ready to do whatever she needed to provide for her child.

Just after lunch one afternoon, Hannah felt an unsettling feeling in her stomach. She found it hard to breathe. Worrying, Hannah shouted for her mum. As she was telling her mother what she felt like, Kelly made her a cup of tea as she knew it would settle her. Giving the teabag one last stir, Kelly asked Hannah to pass her the milk. Hannah nodded, trying to take her mind off the pain. She took a deep breath and pushed herself up. As soon as she stood, she felt a warm sensation dribble down her legs and looked down.

"Err, mum I think I have just weed on the floor," Hannah yelled in disgust.

Kelly chuckled under her breath knowing what had just happened. "C'mon love, I better be getting you to the hospital, your waters just broke."

By the time they reached the hospital, Hannah was in a lot of pain, clutching at anything she could. Kelly had phoned ahead so the hospital was able to get Hannah a bed ready on the maternity ward. In her room, Hannah could not even take her trousers off for the pain, so Kelly was tasked with the job. While Hannah focused on her breathing, the nurse put a mask on her face, for gas and air to reduce the pain. While puffing away and letting out the occasional grunt, the nurse checked to see if Hannah was ready.

The gas and air kept the pain at bay for around ten minutes, but it kept coming back with a vengeance as she screamed. The nurse went to take another measurement, she was met with a top of a head. Hannah was ten centimetres dilated.

"Now Hannah," said the nurse, as she put some rubber gloves on. "Take some deep breaths for me."

Hannah grabbed her mother's hand.

"Can you push for me, please."

Hannah pushed and continued to do so with all the energy she could muster up for the next five minutes. She was weak, she was tired, she was drained. Hannah gave off one final push as she cried with all her might, she was answered by the cries of a baby. The nurse wrapped the baby in a white towel and passed it to Hannah while telling her it was a boy. Hannah hugged her son as she cried. She was so happy, he was the most beautiful thing she had ever laid eyes on. She told the boy that his dad would be so proud of him.

Looking up at the sky, Hannah cried in relief, "Sean, I would like you to meet our son, King Sean Jr Barkly.

TO BE CONTINUED . . .

About the Author

Anthony L. Olaseinde has been fighting against knife crime in South Yorkshire for over three years with his award-winning anti-knife crime campaign #KEEP SHEFFIELD STAINLESS.

Alongside running a business and completing his university course: gaining a Bachelor's in Engineering with first-class Honours in Computer and Network Engineering and proceeding on to gain a Masters of Science with Distinction in Advanced Computer Networks.

Despite his academic success, Anthony decided he wanted to share his experiences with young people and encourage them to be the best version of themselves. Consequently, he created Always an Alternative, a non-profit company aimed at challenging the mindset of young people.

I would love to know what you thought of One Knife Many Lives.

You can write a review with your thoughts here:

- Amazon

- Instagram

- Twitter

- Facebook

Connect with the author:

Instagram: @antzjourney

Twitter: @antzjourney

Facebook: Big Ant

About Always An Alternative

We are a non-profit organisation created with the ultimate aim of reducing serious youth violence: knife crime, gun crime and gangs by engaging the youthful minds of today. We deem education as vital in order to achieve our goals offering a variety of educational routes to inform young people about the risk of serious youth violence.

All routes have two main topics, knife crime and gun crime/gangs and start with an engagement session to allow students to decide some of the non-mandatory topics of decision.

Interested?

Connect with the cause:

Website: www.alwaysanalternative.org.uk

Email: info@alwaysanalternative.org.uk

Instagram: @aaamindset

Facebook: Always An Alternative